POWERFUL, CLASSY & SUPERNATURAL

The Nature of Apostolic & Prophetic People

I0539761

'A PEOPLE OF HIS FIRE'

Apostle Cardwell L Nyaungwa
DCE, MCE, MBs, BTh

1

''For all creation awaits with eager anticipation for the manifestation of the sons of God''
Romans 8:19

Here We Are – Apostle Dr CL Nyaungwa
JAN 2018

''For the creation was subjected to futility — not willingly, but because of Him who subjected it — in the hope that the creation itself will also be set free from the bondage of corruption into the glorious freedom of God's children. For we know that the whole creation has been groaning together with labor pains until now'' vs20-23.

'A People of His fire'

This fire is going to manifest in your life after you finish reading this book. You also must start doubting the devil's messages and start believing only God's voice to you. You are on your way to manifest as a son of God. Enjoy your read.........

COPYRIGHT

ISBN: 978-0-620-79759-7

www.GileadVESTcorporation.com

+27 71 849 5243 - International (voice, message, app)

P.O Box 1174 Isando. Kempton Park. 1600. South Africa

gileadVEST@gmail.com

PRAISE FOR THIS BOOK

My, my, my, oh my, to be honest, I have not written anything like this before, a book packed with revelation after revelation, doctrine and the heavy presence of the divine in every page.

Author

The Mystery, Miracle Talk Show, was a vivid book narrating the works that God has done; now Dr Cardwell takes us to walk with that same God of miracles, in the same miracles and power. This is a must read for spiritual shift.

Eugene Elliot, Papua New Guinea

Thank you my friend for teaching these things to us. It is indeed a heritage for all apostles and prophets out there.

Apostle Addo, Randfontein, Johannesburg

Having known Dr Cardwell for a couple of years, I have come to accept that he is a true man of God just by interacting and listening to his approach to Kingdom business. This book has come at the right time to define and explain our nature as apostolic and prophetic people.

Prophet Don – Kempton Park

I couldn't put the copy down when I first got hold of Apostle Cardwell's Classic, this book is a must read for every Bible Believing Christian, lives are bound to turn around with this magnificent tool for Apostolic and Prophetic people.

Vicky Violet Kathrin - Queensland

ACKNOWLEDGEMENTS

Forever grateful; I want acknowledge the hand of my Lord El Shaddai – Adonai-Shammah for inspiration to teach and the revelation to turn these sermons into a book.

Secondly, to my lovely wife who has stood by me in my many years of failings, and falling forward to this day. Love and Thanks.

Inspiration and encouragement of my friends Dr. Fred Nana Biney (USA), Bishop James Tshenkeng (SA) on doctrine, Bishop Connex Kadhumah a man of the word, Kenneth Copeland Ministries SA -faith bank, babamukuru G. Gosha – a gifted Barnabas, Rev Onias Steve Tapera, Dr Ernest, Pastor Lameck those daily devotionals, pastor Mac Mateke, Apostle Siyaphambili Moyo a true friend.

COAN Gilead RSA, Zimbabwe and Pakistan- your prayers are sustaining dad in exploits and my spiritual father Rev Leo Malvas and mum Emelda Tsumba, even one word in six months carries me through.

DEDICATION

To my wife Mabel, and our children Faith-Rumbidzai, Mufaro-Hadassah and Hannah-Matigonera, who have to bear with me doing ministry, and many times it has not been smooth sailing for the family due my devotion to these matters of the Kingdom. You are my inspiration.

Church of All Nations, Gilead International Ministries, you are my reason for these exploits.

And to all who are my sons in the Lord, this is for you a gift for eternity.

TABLE OF CONTENTS

INTRODUCTION

An Apostolic people: *Powerful, Classy and Supernatural*! It sounds proud – why not? Over-confident - why not? Boasting – why not? It's our being in God; He has elevated us at salvation such that our boasting is not in ourselves, but in Him. What do we mean when we talk of an apostolic people? What differentiates them from people of other faiths and non believers? Can we really say with certainty that there are an apostolic people in each generation or rather that we have a generation that can be set apart as an apostolic people and not be in error? Is it godly to classify these people as *Powerful, Classy* and *Supernatural* as ascribed to in this book?

Let us start by answering these questions faithfully from an evangelical Pentecostal perspective since these are the very people who are more open to apostolic convictions. This automatically creates a problem for ceassasionists and conservatives, but we have no apologies to make in defining and promoting our apostolic convictions. As an apostle I know and am convinced I owe the saints this much as regards Christendom. Defining apostolic people, they are *Powerful*: that's dominant, important, significant, leading, prominent, and high-ranking, this sums up the power aspect. They are *Classy*; elegant, stylish, chic, fashionable, tasteful, refined, exclusive, sophisticated and up-market. Wow! Thirdly *Supernatural*: paranormal, mystic, ghostly, uncanny, weird, eerie, magical and unnatural.[1]

The term Apostolic or Prophetic People is a very deep biblical connotation. It is God who has set His people apart from the time of the patriarchs. He seem to prefer His people, separate, distinct and elegant. A look at these scriptures will help us embrace the theology of election and separation. There are various echoes in the New
Testament
to support the doctrine of election. We are in line when we say we are God's special people.

1 Peter 2:9
''But ye are a chosen generation, a royal priesthood, an holy nation, a peculiar people; that ye should shew forth the praises of him who hath called you out of darkness into his marvelous light: Which in time past were not a people, but are now the people of God: which had not obtained mercy, but now have obtained mercy''

The implications in this text; one that there are a people God has chosen among the

---

[1] Thesaurus, English dictionary, United States in public online domain

8

many unto whom He ordains royal priesthood. He also makes them a holy nation, and a peculiar people, that's too much favor right! The text also tells us that in time past these elect were not a people, implying that those who have not entered the covenant are not a people; more like not alive. There is a deep chasm between the people of God and unbelievers though we may reside in the same house. As if election only is not enough check out the following passages for distinct features of these apostolic people.

Deut 8:6-9

''For thou art an holy people unto the Lord thy God: the Lord thy God hath chosen thee to be a special people unto himself, above all people that are upon the face of the earth. The Lord did not set his love upon you, nor choose you, because ye were more in number than any people; for ye were the fewest of all people: But because the Lord loved you, and because he would keep the oath which he had sworn unto your fathers, hath the Lord brought you out with a mighty hand, and redeemed you out of the house of bondmen, from the hand of Pharaoh king of Egypt. Know therefore that the Lord thy God, he is God, the faithful God, which keepeth covenant and mercy with them that love him and keep his commandments to a thousand generations''

In **Luke 18:7** we hear this, *''And shall not God avenge his own elect, which cry day and night unto him, though he bear long with them? I tell you that he will avenge them speedily''* It is like God has highly favored, and placed a hedge around His own people. He has really separated them for His own and He will take care of them. These are advantages of the apostolic and prophetic people.

And by apostolic and prophetic we refer to believers who live out their in-living faith the same way the early church did under the leadership of the early apostles. The Apostles are God's sent messengers; they are called out to be pioneers of valiant faith deeds. They exhibit daring faith in the midst of challenges. They go where no one has been to, exhibit daring faith and they lay ground-works on top of rocks etc. In a nutshell, they live out their faith to the fullest. They live on the edge, sacrifice is their watchword. These are people sold out to the cause of Christ; unwavering in their commitment to the call of faith.

Apostolic living is not simple; it's about living the standard of life set by the early church; nothing beats that early church in spiritual dynamic. The early church had convictions that make today's church a living joke: they dared all that scripture entails and reaped the harvest. Their allegiance to Christ made them vulnerable, yes exposed to dangers, made them targets of the enemy, but also vivid and dynamic benefactors of the miraculous grace and many things that today's church can only yearn for. They stood for what they believed and could even die for Christ.

Apostle Paul said, "Are they ministers of Christ? (I speak as a fool) I am more; in labors more abundant, in stripes above measure, in prisons more frequent, in deaths oft. Of the Jews five times received I forty stripes save one. Thrice was I beaten with rods, once was I stoned, thrice I suffered shipwreck, a night and a day I have been in the deep; In journeyings often, in perils of waters, in perils of robbers, in perils by mine own countrymen, in perils by the heathen, in perils in the city, in perils in the wilderness, in perils in the sea, in perils among false brethren; In weariness and painfulness, in watchings often, in hunger and thirst, in fastings often, in cold and nakedness. Beside those things that are without, that which cometh upon me daily; the care of all the churches. Who is weak, and I am not weak? Who is offended, and I burn not?'' **2 Cor 11:24-28.**

This is man who we might all attest was the greatest apostle of his generation. Ours is no different zone; we can ride the same levels of spirituality and victorious living. But the reason we are so far from that domain is that we have substituted a lot of Christological truths with doctrines we don't even understand ourselves; we have cheapened the very altar for ease of religiosity. We are not willing to live sacrificial lives. We need a new call to return back to the foundations if we are to experience the same power and presence that our faith ancestors encountered.

From a layman's point of view all believers are saints of God. However an investigation into each man's faith will tell us a different narrative. All those who are blood washed deserve the title of saints unto our God, yes, but it does not end with the washing of blood; there are elements accompanying Christendom. Let Holy Spirit and the Bible teach each man a satisfactory walk of faith. We will share ahead some elements that make up these apostolic people. These are a people called to be worshippers and exhibitors of God's power

'Spare yourself the theology and go down on your knees in adoration' that was an answer given to a new music member in March 2017 when she asked me, "Papa vangu, 'What is worship'' can it be differentiated from praise? These two words confuse me. 'Stop seeking wisdom and start seeking after God; He can be found in deep worship. Not knowing, but loving; the more you love God is the more you shall know Him. This knowledge is a product of intimate worship. What again is worship? It is to feel in your heart and express in some appropriate manner a humbling but delightful sense of admiring awe and astonished wonder and overpowering love in the presence of that most ancient Mystery, that Majesty which philosophers call the First Cause, but which we call Our Father Which Art in Heaven[2].

To worship God is to recognize his worth or worthiness; to look God-ward, and to acknowledge in all appropriate ways the value of what we see. The Bible calls this activity "glorifying God" or "giving glory to God," and views it as the ultimate end, and from one point of view, the whole duty of man **(Ps. 29:2; 96:6; 1 Cor. 10:31)**, Westminster Catechism[3]. As such, are apostolic people; worshippers of the True God in Spirit and in Truth.

Scripture views the glorifying of God as a six-fold activity:

> ➢ Praising God for all that He is and all his achievements;
> ➢ Thanking Him for his gifts and his goodness to us;
> ➢ Asking Him to meet our own and others' needs;
> ➢ Offering Him our gifts, our service, and ourselves;
> ➢ Learning of Him from his word, read and preached,
> ➢ And obeying His voice; telling others of his worth, both by public confession and testimony to what he has done for us[4].

Thus we might say that the basic statements that formulate true worship are these: "Lord, you are wonderful", Lord I love you, "Thank you, Lord"; "Please Lord"; "Take this, Lord"; "Yes, Lord"; "Listen everybody!" I lift my hands in awe, 'Rise up in honor everybody! And all the virtues of human exchange that puts every focus upon the divine, nothing else will do.

This then is worship in its largest sense: petition as well as praise, preaching as well as prayer, hearing as well as speaking, actions as well as words, obeying as well as offering, loving people as well as loving God. However, the primary acts of worship are those which focus on God directly - and we must not imagine that work for God in the world is a substitute for direct fellowship with him in praise and prayer and adoration.

A report is given of Neil Marten, a member of the British Parliament, was once giving a group of his constituents a guided tour of the Houses of Parliament. During the course of the visit, the group happened to meet Lord Hailsham; then Lord Chancellor, wearing all the regalia of his office. Hailsham recognized Marten among the group and

---

[2] AW Tozer, In Pursuit of the Most Holy
[3] The Westminster Catechism is an instructor book for Anglican Worship Services
[4] SWN online blogs 2017

cried, "Neil!" Not daring to question or disobey the "command," the entire band of visitors promptly fell to their knees! Likewise, going on our knees is apostolic practice; a virtue of paying homage to the divine.

What does this have to do with apostolic people in worship! Worship is the submission of all our nature to God. It is the quickening of conscience by His holiness; the nourishment of mind with His truth; the purifying of imagination by His beauty; the opening of the heart to His love; the surrender of will to His purpose - and all of this gathered up in adoration, the most selfless emotion of which our nature is capable and therefore the chief remedy for that self-centeredness which is our original sin and the source of all actual sin. A conscious recognition of who God is leads to earnest and perfect worship.

Barclay quotes William Temple, the renowned Archbishop of Canterbury[5], as defining worship as quickening the conscience by the holiness of God, feeding the mind with the truth of God, purging the imagination by the beauty of God, opening the heart to the love of God, and devoting the will to the purpose of God. This is ultimate; when the conscience is quickened; the inner eyes and ears open up to the reality of the divine; they open up to a world anew, a shock of sorts in emotion that a 'Hallelujah' will not be a conscious act, but an impromptu and perfect response.

My college lecturer gave this story while teaching worship to his Masters Class; ''the citizens of Feldkirch, Austria, didn't know what to do. Napoleon's massive army was preparing to attack. Soldiers had been spotted on the heights above the little town, which was situated on the Austrian border. A council of citizens was hastily summoned to decide whether they should try to defend themselves or display the white flag of surrender.

It happened to be Easter Sunday, and the people had gathered in the local church. The pastor rose and said, "Friends, we have been counting on our own strength, and apparently that has failed. As this is the day of our Lord's resurrection, let us just ring the bells, have our services as usual, and leave the matter in His hands. We know only our weakness, and not the power of God to defend us." The council accepted his plan and the church bells rang. The enemy, hearing the sudden peal, concluded that the Austrian army had arrived during the night to defend the town. Before the service ended, the enemy broke camp and left''.

Therein is the power of worship defined; there is no better example. When we worship we are in the realm of surrender. And in the realm of surrender great things happen

---

[5] Church History

with the divine. God seeks and values the gifts we bring Him-gifts of praise, thanksgiving, service, and material offerings. In all such giving at the altar we enter into the highest experiences of fellowship. But the gift is acceptable to God in the measure to which the one who offers it is in fellowship with Him, in character and conduct; and the test of this is in our relationships with our fellow men. We are thus charged to postpone giving to God until right relationships are established with others. Could the neglect of this be the explanation of the barrenness of our worship? **(Matt 5:24)**

It is therefore imperative that the ultimate deep, the ultimate sacrifice, the ultimate offering and the ultimate endeavor of the apostolic people is the part whereby worship and honor is ascribed unto the Lord. Let worship stem from the right attitude and the right mindset and the whole world will know who really, are the sons of God. We can set the universe alight with the Glory of God! Let us raise those voices in praise and deep worship.

CHAPTER 1
FOUNDATION OF THE APOSTLES and PROPHETS

Our current theme is the position of enlightened saints, whose understanding has received the revelation that they are an apostolic seed. These people know their position in God, a position that many 'called' may fail to comprehend because they may have received a man-made discipleship or another gospel especially in our age of artificial doctrines. The church (saints) is built upon the word of the Apostles and Prophets as Apostle Paul by the Spirit of God shares in **Ephesians 2:20**. This scripture carries weight in the heart of the apostle as his primary call was to establish churches as an evangelist, apostle and prophet. It cannot be denied that he possessed all the gifts given in to the church by Christ according to Ephesians 4:11.

The Church Foundations of Eph 2:20

Building an apostolic & Prophetic people

APOSTLES   PROPHETS

JESUS CHRIST & THE BLODDY CROSS

It's Jesus' Church; We Are His Possession!

There are many theoretical suppositions that ministers and theologians use to explain the text of **Ephesians 4:11**. It is important to note that God only want us to make of primary importance the fact that Jesus gave gifts for the equipping of the saints. The politics of greater gifts and the grading of the same becomes our own theology. Others use the five fingers to typify the five gifts, others use the law of First Mention, yet others still just treat their own calling as the eminent one or try to explain the others equally as theirs so that they don't appear inferior in calling.

All this is man stuff; it's no God debate. However, what is written has been written for our benefit, so as the apostle Paul puts the Apostles and Prophets at an elevated level; it is up to us to study the scriptures to reveal the heart and mind of the Apostle in that context and come to a godly conclusion regarding the mysteries. Here is an overview of the office of Apostle and Prophet. Scripture exhort us to study to show ourselves approved of God and be workman (servants) who do not need to be ashamed of the Gospel, but those who rightly divide the truth and correctly handling it.

- Jesus has called, serviced, graced, and anointed His servants the Apostles and Prophets to execute divine work; on a level different from most of the other spiritual gifts.
- Therefore, He, Jesus becomes the cornerstone of our confession, our faith, our service, our ministries, our churches, our denominations etc.
- The Apostle and prophet become the foundation upon which Jesus is building His church according to scripture;
- Apart from me you can do nothing **(JESUS) John 15:5**) the servants and the saints are all alive only in Christ, it's all about Jesus, from the onset and ultimately: JESUS.

This explains Why the Apostle Paul gave us apostolic/prophetic and not pastoral or evangelistic foundations! Surely the great apostle had a God ordained message for all generations in this. Let us look at **Eph 2:9-22** as the heart of the great apostle pounds with conviction at the establishment of a living Body of Christ.

(i). "Not of works, lest any man should boast. For we are his workmanship, created in Christ Jesus to do good works,

(ii). at that time ye were without Christ, being aliens from the commonwealth of Israel, and strangers from the covenants of promise, having no hope, and without God in the world:

(iii) But now in Christ Jesus ye who sometime were far off are made nigh by the blood of Christ.

(iv) For he is our peace;

(v) For through him we both have access by one Spirit unto the Father.

(vi) Now therefore ye are no more strangers and foreigners, but fellow citizens with the saints, and of the household of God;

(vii) Built upon the foundation of the apostles and prophets, Jesus Christ himself being the chief corner stone.

We are not trying to elevate any gift above the other as that will be a theological disaster, but as the Biblical law stands, the callings are not equal. Yes, it is Christ who calls but we have different levels of grace, all working together in harmony to execute that divine mandate placed upon our lives. Indeed the apostle heads the gift list of **Ephesians 4:11,** and follows the much confused gift of prophecy (as an office not the function). We do not have time to attend all the gifts one by one but according to the law of First Mention, the Apostles and Prophets seem to have been elevated and apostle Paul by the Spirit of God concurred in **Ephesians 2:22**. Now back to our text, let us precept by precept explore the framework that builds on to an apostolic people.

"Not of works, lest any man should boast is an indicator that what God builds no man should claim to author it. It is man's tendency to want to claim the glory, even in matters that he knows nothing about. God would not have that for He originally said, ''All Glory is mine''. And indeed there is no other glory except His. Paul at one point says if any man would boast; let him boast in that he knows the Lord. A sobering thought for wayward saints. Salvation is of God through Christ alone.

No human hand can claim any part thereof to the mystery of salvation. God has extended His hand throughout the ages to rebellious mankind that he be restored to a life of communion and fellowship with his Maker. But man has been apt to say, 'No' to God's hand extended in mercy, and therein lays the problem. However, God who is rich in mercy; gracious and compassionate such that He never withdrew his hand from the invitation to Adam's brood to return to covenant life.

Apostle Paul continues, "For we are his workmanship: ''Workmanship sounds like a word for partners, workers together in a certain or specific project. We are His workmanship; yea, we work with God in Christ for God. Our labors are delegated as a commission; we are subjects and yet co-workers at the same time. The word workmanship speaks also of skill; of ability and competence, meaning we have the same skill, ability and competence with God as regards matters of the kingdom. It is not wholly correct to set man as objects in God's eye: the apostolic generation know there is more. We are created in His image.

Our role of stewardship can also not be underestimated; the word says, ''moreover it is be befitting that a steward found faithful'' **(1 Cor 4:2)** The people of His fire work in faithful adherence to His word. We are stewards yes, but working with God, not working as the unfaithful servant who hid his talent in the ground without the knowledge that 'a steward owns what the master owns'. The aspect of Workmanship should indeed push us further in knowledge and skill so that we do not mess up in the

partnership we have with our God. We have been given everything we need for the work: we have an anointing to carry us through life and godliness. ''Grace be to you, and peace, from God our Father, and from the Lord Jesus Christ.
Blessed be the God and Father of our Lord Jesus Christ, who hath blessed us with all spiritual blessings in heavenly places in Christ'' **Eph 1:3.**

We are without excuse if we do not function as an apostolic people. Modern heresy is an extension of early heresy; there is nothing new under the sun. Any denial of apostolic grace is a theological misnomer, we need to rise up in faith and conviction and claim our rightful place in the kingdom of God. We are an apostolic people; if you are deprived of such a freedom of faith, examine your religion. The Body of Christ is massive that no single man can claim hold of any other's soul without being found out, its sorcery. This book has come to liberate the apostolic generation to go out there in confidence and faith and turn the world upside down in exhibiting and practicing genuine faith.

Apostles and prophets play a key role in the lives of apostolic believers. It has always been God's plan to touch the lives of His people through His ordained servants. Apostle Paul in the text concludes with a matter we believe is very crucial to the well being of the Body of Christ. The apostle's doctrine, their way of life; both of the early church and today, their allegiance to the Gospel and unwavering commitment to the cause of Christ makes them the NT patriarchs. Their word as an anchor resonates with a confirmation of Christological truths. They are Jesus called, Jesus graced and Jesus sent to do divine work.

The word apostle in original languages means the sent one with Jesus being the first and Greater Apostle sent from heaven to earth. He is the Chief Apostle; the stone that the builders rejected which has now been made the cornerstone. There is an element of agreement that Apostles are undisputed; the ones whom God has really called have a different level of spiritual function than most would love to agree. Some of the queries regarding apostolic work are not justified; there is grace for miracles, grace for exploits and grace to do what no one else is doing than those who are content with the ordinary and start querying the extraordinary. In **Isaiah 8:18**, the word says, "I and the children God has given me are for signs and wonders in Israel'. It is upon every true apostolic leader to teach the truth that power is granted in various measures to all the elect, as the leader goes so goes the followers! God will help us understand this.

One of my close apostle friends always say in defiance, "Apostle havapererwi"[6] that's Shona wording for 'an apostle will never run out of ideas or steam! Indeed the call to pirotage, pioneering the work of God in seemingly impractical zones and the grace to address doors and gates unhithetho touched, sets the apostle apart. From my experience of the apostolic life, there is a shift from ordinary Christian living to extraordinary realms. The apostolic seed always triumphs creating eternal testimonies about the power of Christ.

No matter the battles and challenges, the apostolic seed, the seed of the righteous always gets a way through. The covenant they have with God is an awesome partnership; you touch me you have touched my God, you touch my God you have touched me and God is not shamed to call them, "My people'' The apostolic people have a serious covenant with their God sustained through faith in God, faith in Jesus and faith in the person of Holy Spirit. There is rich reward in trusting God and believing his prophets: **2 Chronicles 20:20**. Always remember in this book we are referring to faithful apostles and prophets who stick to the word and divine inspiration other than the modern day heretic who thrives on charm and charisma while not upholding the minimum ethical and spiritual standards.

It is each individual believer's, church board and leadership team's responsibility to always test, analyze and examine the spirits at work in us Apostles so that we will not lead them astray in these churches and Christian organizations. Apostle John's purpose of that famous verse, "Test the spirits" **1 John 4:1** is a sure indicator that God want us to deal with any deviation from correct doctrine in spiritual wisdom and before it catches the ears of the sheep.

We therefore make a conscious decision to un-follow the false prophet or apostle, to save ourselves from their poisonous doctrines. It is every single individual's responsibility to defend the faith according to **Jude 3**; we can all do this by refusing false doctrine, and promoting the whole counsel of the word of God in our lives. Apostolic people love Christ, they obey His commands, and they love the brethren, and know their limitations as stewards of the holy calling and servants of the Kingdom. They are like the people of Berea, a rare group of disciples who loved the word so much that after every single service, they gathered to verify the message of the Apostles and to embrace further the mysteries of the kingdom. They had no time to waste like our entertainment crazy generation which has created spiritual zombies both in and outside the church.

---

[6] Apostle G Gosha, Founder: Sure Foundation Ministries

CHAPTER 2
THE APOSTLE AND HIS PEOPLE
'Enduring Partnerships'

The call of the Old Testament patriarchs was to lead the chosen nation in the ways of Jehovah. Others started the Exodus while others managed the sacred link between Jehovah and His people, yet still others led the crossing of the Jordan River and the conquest. They all acted both as apostles and prophets of God unto His people. Their main thrust was to sustain the relationship between Jehovah and the Hebrew nation. The New Testament apostle is not exempt from this assignment; Jesus opened the door for all peoples, languages, nationalities and tribes to become God's people through salvation, therefore the same require honest servants of God to lead them in the ways of Jehovah. Apostles lead as God granted them multiple gifts in one vessel for the sole purpose of maintaining the covenant. There are enduring partnerships and gift linkages requiring unity and harmony among all saints to deliver a complete and fulfilled church to God.

Our role as NT apostles is to change the world for God, by equipping the saints for the works of ministry. When saints are equipped, it becomes possible to change our world with the love, knowledge and the word of Christ. Souls have to be won to Christ: we can do no other. As spiritual fathers we minister the grace through teaching and preaching; we engage every office in the land to institute the fear of God. We have been given the power to invoke territorial graces; no nation shall be immune to our gospel and to our God. It is our challenge and task to expand the Kingdom. It is our call as apostles and prophets to make a positive impact for Christ; and, as we do so, our children will also function on higher ground; these are the ones we are calling in this book 'apostolic people'.

Apostolic people play their part in the partnership they have with their apostle. They support in every way; financially, morally, spiritually to all God honoring programs presented by the apostles and even give anonymously to the ministry. Their sharing with those in need also becomes a holy act. Through church programs or individually they sustain the revelation. Giving to God with no expectation for payback is the highest form of giving. The lowest is when we give to make some bargain with the divine on our needs. Those who stand with their apostles will in no wise go without God noticing their spiritual endeavors.

He will invoke His blessing, whether expected or not, and every act of obedience shall be met with commensurate divine response. Any sacrifice given for a worthwhile ministry project does not only relieve the apostle; but surely touches God's heart. There is also a ministry that has created controversy among the unenlightened; giving to the man of God. We will explore ahead some daring feats of giving to the man of God as a way out of extreme starvation in the land of the patriarchs.

"And Elijah said unto her, Fear not; go, and do as thou hast said: but make me thereof a little cake first, and bring it unto me and after make for thee and for thy son. For thus saith the Lord God of Israel, ''The barrel of meal shall not waste, neither shall the cruse of oil fail, until the day that the Lord sendeth rain upon the earth. And she went, and did according to the saying of Elijah; and she, and he, and her house, did eat many days. And the barrel of meal wasted not, neither did the cruse of oil fail, according to the word of the Lord, which he spake by Elijah" **Kings 17: 13-16) KJV**[7]

''The Word of Elijah, the Word Of Elijah, O' That The Word of My Mouth be as Powerful''

The word of Elijah, seem to carry weight and authority wherever he went. Would that be that God's sent ones have been appointed to an office elevated than man would want to accept? The attendance due to a king must not supersede the honor due to the man of God, and by man of God I am indeed still referring to faithful men and women of God serving in holiness and obedience to the word. They are worth any honor in doubles as long as they stick to the Holy Book. **1 Tim 5:17.**

How mysterious the ways of God: man as servants carry authority and power liberally granted by the divine. The Elijahs of old can still have their copy in our generation if only we would dare. The word of Elijah, the word of Elijah! That was a common statement among the Hebrews during Elijah's ministry and it continued during his successor Elisha's ministry. It must not stop now; the man of God has to stand the ground and prove that God is the same yesterday, today and forever! **Heb 13:8.**[8] The grace of God is available from generation to generation to them that fear Him. Elijah represents the man of God and messengers of heaven in all generations; he was the type. God uses His servants to execute His divine plan on earth. They serve as his vassals to the Kingdom. The plan cascades to every born again believer appointed at salvation to be ambassadors for Christ. The assignments are given in commensurate to the anointing (grace) received. We should note that there are spiritual levels in as much as there are various levels elsewhere. And God will not allow anyone of His children to go through what they are not able to bear; this is a golden nugget of Christendom.

[7] KJV is in public domain
[8] NIV is public domain

The apostle carries a higher calling with weightier kingdom responsibilities. The issue of responsibilities thus humbles us to embrace the stewardship mode; for its all for God by God. We need to know our God; Elijah knew his God and had a clear relationship with him. What God did with his Elijah and His Elisha, cannot be comprehended by the human mind; they say even in death Elisha continued to resurrect dead people.

2 Kings 13:21,

"And it came to pass, as they were burying a man, that, behold, they spied a band of men; and they cast the man into the sepulcher of Elisha: and when the man was let down, and touched the bones of Elisha, he revived, and stood up on his feet" KJV

Long dead was the prophet but God decided to activate his anointing even in that rotten body, the power was still at work. This is a mystery of the apostolic people; resurrections can happen any moment. Just be careful how you treat when you are with these people, their God is a livewire. When we talk about the anointing, it's not cleverly invented fables; but the reality of God's power at work in us.

Back to our key text of this section, we can safely say that Elisha and the Sidonian woman both belonged to Elijah: they were the apostle's people. Elijah's anointing was given in double to his servant Elisha. The God of Elijah fed Elijah's people a full year in the season drought and starvation. How rewarding faithful service to the man of God can be. Elisha worked for Elijah before he worked for God. These two Apostles/ prophets changed the cause of faith forever; from being fed by the ravens to raising the dead, the bald headed Elisha calling upon wild hyenas to deal with erring young girls in the hills of Samaria and the ordeal of crossing a heavily flooded Jordan twice repeated.

"As the Lord God liveth, before whom I stand, there shall be neither dew nor rain these years, but according to my word." A prophet causes the judgment. Elijah literally acts like God in that episode. He continues, ''Fetch me, I pray thee, a little water in a vessel, that I may drink" and as she went to fetch, he called again as though the Lord would gradually and gently prepare her mind for the great test that He was bringing. "Bring me also, I pray thee, a morsel of bread in thine hand."

Then it was that her spirit broke, we can only imagine. The water she would spare, but the bread was too much as yet for her hospitality to venture. How pathetic the cry of her distress, she responds in familiar fashion; "As the Lord thy God liveth, I have not a cake, but a handful of meal in a barrel, and a little oil in a cruse: and, behold, I am gathering two sticks, that I may go in and dress it for me and my son, that we may eat it, and die." Well organized was the poor widow's plea, graced with all the correct words, just like the excuse often haunting the spiritually untrained eye. Does Apostle Elijah give up then?

No, the ministry has to be completed despite the obstacles. Then comes the mighty message of faith, "Fear not; go, and do as thou hast said: but make me thereof a little cake first, and bring it unto me, and after make for thee and for thy son. The prophet seems again to take the place of God, a baffling truth that God allows us to act in His behalf in telling and delicate circumstances. Who would quarrel with an authoritative man of God whose works speak for themselves like Elijah!

The declarations continued, ''For thus saith the Lord God of Israel, the barrel of meal shall not waste, neither shall the cruse of oil fail, until the day that the Lord sendeth rain upon the earth. "And she went, and did according to the saying of Elijah; and she, and he, and her house, did eat many days," or other versions say, a full year, "and the barrel of meal wasted not, neither did the cruse of oil fail, according to the word of the Lord, which he spake by Elijah. The mouthpiece so harmoniously woven with the speaker, surely the miracle cannot tarry! My good wife calls it the power of an unending supply that was unlocked by the woman; who would argue! She ate and her whole house, the extended family came in to join the supply. Her sacrifice, deserve acknowledgement, her trust in the God of the Hebrews is a lesson to all of the apostolic people out there willing to learn and trust their God in seemingly hopeless situations. God will come through for those who obey him.

The Value of Word of the Man Of God

Let us look at the value of the man of God and as we go we will spell out the value of the partner to the man of God. We see here an excellent interchange between Elijah and God and the woman. Here is a mystery that conservatives find difficult to accept; Evangelicals are guilty of undermining and the cult n crass abuse and misuse. We can all benefit and hasten the return of our Lord if we would allow scripture to govern our religious activities. The power of God is still the same as it was in Elijah's time; it speaks miracles upon miracles since the time of Isaiah, only our conduct around the holy thing is blocking the move of God in our midst. There is no argument to the word of Christ that, many are called but a few are chosen. It is the same as the oracle of a house with many articles for various uses.
The apostle or prophet have been granted a higher grace level:

- First Elijah shuts the rains, when he got angry with Ahab;

- The word of Elijah became a divine law.

- No rain until at my word:

- The word of the prophet aligned with the divine plan becomes the word of God.

- God enters the scene, For thus saith the Lord, the promise of supply;

- In as much as the word of God is adopted by the prophet as his own, God intervenes.

- God seems bound by His word, and is affixed to its fruitful realizing, the outcomes bears on his Name and His Glory.

- Until the Lord sendeth rain upon the earth; Elijah shuts, the Lord opens. At first he said until at my word, there shall be no rain. Now he says until the Lord sendeth rain.

What an excellent discourse, what rich harmony, in the deeds of the faithful minister and his God. I can't do without God and I also can't do without my man of God! Would you? The woman in the text had to accept the two centers of power or her hope was gone; Elijah and God worked in harmony so she had to cooperate with the one she was facing. Even nature, climate and the weather obeyed the word of Elijah. God was bound to bring to pass Elijah's words in as much as the prophet was bound to boldly speak forth the word of God. Even today, our word carries varying degrees of power: that in as much as the apostle adopts God's words to be his own, God honors it.

In the ministry of the saints to the man of God, the beauty of Elijah and the Sidonian woman narrative is compelling;
a. We have here a beautiful picture of fellowship in service and Apostolic work, the man of the word and a woman of faith.
   b. For a whole year this humble and lowly woman supported a prophet all alone to show us what faith can still do through us in the Master's work.
   c. He who shares with a prophet in the name of a prophet
   (*consciously*) will receive the prophet's reward. **(Mathew 10:41)**
Of ministry partnerships heaven cannot ignore, my God is not a man that He should lie neither is He the son of man that he should change His mind. He has spoken and He will do it. As apostolic people I entreat you to support ministry and the man of God. If God remains silent over you after giving to the man of God, please call me I will refund you the full cost of this book times ten.

d. The background story keeps making noise; God might just as well have still continued to support Elijah by the ravens of the wilderness, but He wanted to establish this precedent and leave this pattern for other Apostles in all the coming ages.

e. As an apostolic person, do you personally or your business support Ministry? In the apostle's work you have direct benefits of partnership, and in soul-winning you have no direct benefit but still you are giving, therein lies a true test of your giving attitude!

f. Do you have a program of ministry support? Or a personal or family budget for ministry support? Until this is aligned, you will work so hard and harvest little, eat too much still not get full.
We can refer you to **Haggai 1:5-10**.

''Now therefore thus saith the Lord of hosts; Consider your ways. Ye have sown much, and bring in little; ye eat, but ye have not enough; ye drink, but ye are not filled with drink; ye clothe you, but there is none warm;
and he that earneth wages earneth wages to put it into a bag with holes.
Thus saith the Lord of hosts; Consider your ways.
Go up to the mountain, and bring wood, and build the house;
and I will take pleasure in it, and I will be glorified, saith the Lord.
Ye looked for much, and, lo, it came too little; and when ye brought it home, I did blow upon it. Why? saith the Lord of hosts. Because of mine house that is waste, and ye run every man unto his own house. Therefore the heaven over you is stayed from dew, and the earth is stayed from her fruit''

Support ministry, the church, finance missionary work and be there for the man of God or Haggai 1 will be applicable to your own life. We can't say more than what the word is clearly teaching here. We as servants of God need you to believe in us; I for one can confirm that there are countless saints who believed in me, in God's call upon my life when I was like zero, a nothing. Those people supported me in the heat and in cold; when down and when firing from all cylinders; when none trusted my dreams and vision they stood with me and exploits where done in enormous measure.

Even today I have very good, blessed and capable friends and partners at COAN Gilead who support my vision and I am so thankful to the Lord for them. There are some who never bother to look at my work again once I left my old denomination of twenty-two years. It seems like I made enemies when God gave me a different direction and vision to my former church, but there are godly sons and daughters who have stood by me and believed in my call to this day, it has not been a disappointment but a rewarding journey with exploits coming through at God speeds. I owe it to them, I also owe it to those from outside Gilead International Ministries who take their time to think and pray about me, about COAN and about my family. No man of God can survive a week without faithful saints supporting him in various ways possible. Partners and church members, saints and leadership teams, do not lose heart when the

24

world changes its doctrine, remain true to him who is the same yesterday, today and forever and your efforts shall not be in vain. Yes scrutinize our doctrine, scan through our conduct if we are meeting the scriptural standards, correct us when we go wrong – don't dump us, and stand with us for God seeks such to be pillars of the Kingdom.

Big business or small, poor or rich, able or disabled, young and old, all must make a decision to support the work of God in any way possible: talents, gifts, finances, moral support, prayer etc. Today a great proportion of the missionary money of the Church comes from people like the widow of Zarephath. I work with an organization for Christian Leadership Development which is an organization for leadership development in third world countries and our major source of funding is from people such as the aged, widows and single mothers who desire to see the knowledge of the Lord spread all over the world as the waters covers the sea. Humble as they are, their individual little contribution consolidate to become dozens of leadership workshops and events each and every year since June 1999.

Do not, therefore, excuse yourself from the responsibility or be discouraged in your efforts because you are humble and poor. God is simply asking, as pastor Ray[9] puts it, "the five barley loaves and two fishes, the two mites that make a farthing, the thing that is "in thine hand," and His power will make it "mighty to the pulling down of strongholds" No-matter how you feign yourself the poorest in the church; give your whole Tithe and decide on your freewill offering either at the beginning of the month or every Saturday night. You can give your Tithe or offering on any day to avoid the fake temptation to use the holy thing for your personal need. The value you put on your offering is for you to decide; the tithe is a divine decree, ten percent. Make your own conclusions about the issue of giving, and see the result, God is not a man that He should lie on oath, **Numbers 23:19**. He has spoken and He will do it I repeat.

The rule remains: 'To whom much have been given, much is expected' **Luke 12:48**. Some rich man fed David and his men when they were at war, no poor man could afford that with the size of the army. Boaz fed Naomi and daughter in law. Much of the great works done by the saints in ministry support cannot be ignored; they carry an important earth responsibility in the functions of the kingdom. As I write this book I had a Couples Dinner to enrich and build great marriages in my church and two rich guys offered to pay the bill for everyone in attendance after the event. I felt so blessed and even proud to have such men in the congregation, and which leader wouldn't?

---

[9] Green Pastures Quiet Waters, Ray Pritchard 1999.

The apostle becomes weak without a strong support base, but strong with enabled support both spiritual and financial. It is a truth that in almost all churches, the few, the rich, carry the many- we cannot do much about it, it is a spiritual reality. However, the Lord and the apostle desire a corporate partnership whereby every soul participates in kingdom expansion. As an Apostle I now understand this applicable to my partners; 'We are because you are'!

CHAPTER 3
A PEOPLE OF SACRIFICE

We have so far learnt that apostolic people are built upon the foundations of the apostles and the prophets and have defined them according to the scriptures. The callings are varied depending on the nature of assignment God had for each one of us at creation. We also agree that the matter can go deeper as saying Kingdom business is the apostle and his people, though being himself a 'vassal' of God.

The next lesson was Elijah and the poor widow where we saw a b*eautiful picture of fellowship in service and apostolic work*. The story taught us that sacrifice opens ''doors'' of ''unending supply'' as my lovely wife puts it. We have also discovered that God uses both the rich and the poor in apostolic ministry support. The poor must not feign inferiority; for even the last and least in the hand can unlock the miracle. All believers can have their say in the matters of the Kingdom in various ways and acts.

Between the widow and death stood a little oil and a little flour, she had spiritual a choice to make. The woman did an extraordinary work that we the rich can be jealous of. On the other hand the rich must also feign to not have at times, the size of the gift is equal to the size of seed you are sowing. The giver of the seed to the sower, knows everything in the purse. For a man reaps what he sows. The quality of the seed (all giving) is measured by the attitude leading to the harvest.

And they said, ''The God of the Hebrews hath met with us: let us go, we pray thee, three days' journey into the desert, and sacrifice unto the Lord our God; lest he fall upon us with pestilence, or with the sword''. We get this from Exodus 5:3, when the chosen people were in bondage under a ruthless ruler. The key point we want to reveal is that sacrifices have to be made at all occasions: either in bondage or in liberty, in poverty or in abundance, in health or in sickness, in good mood or not, let sacrifice due to the King be given without fail. The result rests with the Master.

Sacrifice; Sacrifice. Sacrifice; said the preacher! A sacrifice is not done with a smile on the face; no, that makes it no sacrifice. In any field there is no joy in sacrifices, but the results push man to keep going even in the face of the pain. A critical look at the preparation and training of sportspersons will help us appreciate the content of sacrifice. However hard and difficult it is they push on with various dynamics and even changing from one trainer to the next to make sure the body is thoroughly prepared for competition.

The same with us in spiritual arenas: to sacrifice, we as apostolic and prophetic people have no choice but to do it. We know our Lord has been there; His perfect sacrifice

27

remains the eternal example. Out of very little: His only one child, God decided to show us what sacrificial love can do. We can never better that. Jesus at the cross was the propitiation for our sins. What can we give in response that can match these divine acts? Indeed 'greater love hath no man than this, that one would die for his brethren, but Jesus went to the cross not for brethren, but for rebels; herein is ultimate sacrifice.

The Sidonian woman's act will stand the test of time as a great example, notwithstanding Christ's example foreran by Abraham with Isaac at the mount. This must pass current in the world above and below as a divine standard for sacrificial giving; all or nothing. It cannot be repeated, but as a people He calls His own, we have a responsibility to manifest such daring acts of faith in sacrifice as our spiritual ancestors did. The call is very loud and clear:

A. All or nothing;
B. Abraham must give up his Isaac;
C. Moses must give up his crown;
D. Hannah must give up her boy;
E. The widow must leave her life and her child's, at the mercy of Elijah's God, and surrender even the last link between them and every human possibility of escape from death.
F. What is in your hand? This is the only logical question when attending to the quest for sacrifice. What must you sacrifice so that you will support the work of God?
G. It's ''All'' or ''nothing''.
H. If you do not sacrifice, you become the sacrifice.

Sacrifice supersedes all other types of giving, whatever the agenda, it is the ultimate is Kingdom giving. The laws that govern giving place no limitation upon a sacrifice: scripture gives us some guidelines as regards all other giving:

- To an offering it says, "It shall be given back to you" a good measure, pressed down shaken together shall man place on your hands if you give, Luke 6:38.
- On the Tithe it says, the devourer and the curse shall be broken, Malachi 3:11.
- Celebratory and thanksgivings soothes and nourishes, it's up to your soul.
- To widows and orphans it says you are lending to God.

And what about the sacrifice! There is no limitation to what a sacrifice can do for you. It reaches to the deepest heart of God and causes His countenance to be cast in a new framework towards the giver of the sacrifice. The pain, the agony, the loss and the spiritual emotion heaven cannot ignore. This is a higher level of living; yes, above tithe, the offerings, giving to the needy etc. Sacrifice is a standard measure of what you would be able to do in any other area. Jesus invokes the idea of sacrifice even in daily living; if a man does not carry his cross and follow me, he is not worthy to be my disciple. We may make noise and call it unfair but what's fair in living below the standard he set on the cross? It's all or nothing!

The Mystery of the Sacrifice

- Measured not by what is given, but by what remains:
- If you give and remain with something bigger than given, it therefore is not sacrifice.
- It takes the Spirit of revelation to comprehend.
- A sacrifice speaks louder than our prayers.

The O.T Sacrifice:

- Had no say in the matter at hand; was killed by its owner.
- Was burnt on the fire and the smoke went up to God.
- God loved the smell of burning fat and steak on the altar of sacrifice;
- The person who sacrificed had no share, a sacrifice is unto God, and it's surrendered.

In the N.T times, The Sacrifice Has Changed:

- No more animal burning because of SPCA; unavailability of animals doesn't make it easier either;
- God does not expect any burning sacrifices: animal fat, no, He now wants our hearts and our substance.
- Death was sorted at Calvary as the perfect sacrifice went to the cross;
- N.T sacrifice should be what we value most;
- It has to be something that prick your heart when it goes;
- Be thankful when you build churches, when you sponsor crusades and support fulltime ministers of the gospel.
- Your sacrifice reaches up to God through the funds you give, the houses you avail, the vehicles, your precious time in any department, the prayers etc.

We learn further that the true secret of every sacrifice and service is faith – nothing else will do. The woman developed her faith as Prophet Elijah shared the word of the Lord and his own word with her. Not without a promise from the prophet could she have ventured on this surrender. She had a faith inviting discourse with the man of God and the partnership resulted in a glorious eternal testimony. God did not ask her to give up one world without offering to her another. He is too faithful to demand of us a blind surrender. Only the mystics and false teachers would entertain such.

Even Abraham's mighty sacrifice was not made in blank despair, but in living faith. Yes, he gave up Isaac, but on account of knowing his God; accounting that God was able to raise him up even from the dead". Why are we bringing faith here? The apostolic seed triumph through faith and faith alone. Whatever life throws at them, they through faith emerge victorious. And the power of the covenant demands acts such as sacrifice to become part of the apostolic people's nature. Only biblical faith can enable man-soul to quest for such high mountains of the spiritual life. Without faith it is impossible to please God, **Heb 11:3**. The word is the promise of God; our faith is the only possible link to them. Not blindly following or believing but a living relationship knowing that they that diligently seek Him, shall be rewarded. He is a rewarder, so pursue Him with conviction and intention.

To every sacrifice heaven demands, there is a miracle wrapped in the obedience. Everyone needs a miracle, it is only the type and kind of miracle that differs, and God has them all - Hallelujah! Unfortunately nobody is ever ready to sacrifice; we sacrifice by default, under duress, when it's all gone south. As apostolic people we must understand the power of sacrifice to Christian living. Spend time with your man of God and spend time with God long enough so that you may understand by revelation the secrets, functions and dynamics of the Kingdom.

Your sacrifices should be based on knowledge, on the fear of God and an absolute surrender of personal will to the one who called you. If you do not sacrifice, you will become the sacrifice one day. It is a credit to be able to sacrifice no-matter the circumstances that lead you to the act, but sacrificial obedience to the word or to a revelation is enriching. As bread that is broken, and as wine that is poured out, may God use your life in turning this world for His glory.

CHAPTER 4
POWERFUL, CLASSY, Oh SUPERNATURAL

A God-designed and God-ordained life it is: the life of the apostolic people is a mystery on its own: imagine human beings, being 'in the image of God' and having access to God through the blood of washing and the baptism of purification. The ability to see spiritual things and navigate the spiritual arenas and that ability to 'join with angels and those who have gone before' continue to baffle me, yet I believe. That's right, I believe that we are supernatural, meaning we transcend the natural.

It's supernatural, and out of this visible world, ''for unto which of the angels said he at any time, 'Thou art my Son, this day have I begotten thee? And again, 'I will be to him a Father, and he shall be to me a Son?' Heb 1:5. This scripture is reference to the Lord Jesus, now get this; we have become brothers with Jesus in salvation. When we were born again we 'became' children of God. Whatever applies to Christ, He liberally has granted unto us, his chosen and elect. He is alive inside us.

We will interest ourselves with this supernatural aspect of our being in this section. God literally owns us. 'Thou art mine', you are mine, He thunders in **Isa 43: 1**- ''But now thus saith the Lord that created thee, O Jacob, and he that formed thee, O Israel, Fear not: for I have redeemed thee, I have called thee by thy name; thou art mine. When thou passeth through the waters, I will be with thee; and through the rivers, they shall not overflow thee: when thou walkest through the fire, thou shalt not be burned; neither shall the flame kindle upon thee'' God promises some personal protection upon His elect; He qualifies His ownership of us with assurance of protection even in the midst of possible calamities.

Why is God so much as interested in us? Because we are born of God, we are offspring of God's womb **(2 Cor 5:17)** born again, of God, of the Spirit, begotten by God. We are of a God kind and specie. Apostolic people are a product of the Holy Spirit by whom we cry 'Abba', 'Dad' 'Father' to the living God **Rom 8:14-17**. This sets us apart from the peoples of other religions; not all can say with certainty that they are children of God. In some false religions it's treated as heresy to claim to be a child of God. Not with us, we are the supernatural children of the Most High God. And he has given us everything we need pertaining to life and godliness – perfected!

A close inspection of David's words in **Psalms 18:28 -32** can help us get a clear picture of these supernatural people. (*Doccn's Davidic Deliverance Analysis)* There are physical as well as spiritual wars to be fought; in them all God is an ever-present help to His people. Many a time He says, "I will never leave thee, nor forsake thee" agreeing with David's assured confession. Back to the Psalm, David declares, 'by thee O God' - like a child asking his father to help in a situation. By you oh, Dad ... I can _____says David.'

A closer analysis of what God did for David and what David declared God could do for him is an awesome assurance to the elect. God has a multiple deliverance plan for His people and it is within us to make sure we are aligned. God's position is always right and if we are not wining the battles, trouble is on this side of the covenant. Each man must prepare themselves and position themselves in the right place and at the right place and moment where God is at work. When God decides to turn a man to Himself, the consequences are not always desirable, but he can do anything to get yours and mine attention, even when it hurts.

We will now get back to *Doccn's Davidic Deliverance Analysis*: I have put a few comments on the script in point format to help us focus on the supernatural interventions and we use it in my family to confess our victories from time to time.

BY THEE

OH' GOD.....

1. My Candle is Always Burning
2. My Darkness Is Light in Thee
3. I Can Run Through a Troop;
4. I Can Leap Over a Wall.
5. I Walk Without Stumbling, For His Way is Always Perfect:
6. Nothing Beats His Word; The Word of The Lord is Tried and Tested.
7. In Strength He is A Buckler to All Those That Trust in Him.
8. Undisputed in He; For Who is God Save The Lord? Or Who is A Rock Save Our God?
9. It is God That Girdeth Me With Strength, And Maketh My Way Perfect.
10. He Maketh My Feet Like Hinds' Feet, And Setteth Me Upon My High Places.
11. As For Battles, Not Only Does He Fight For Me, He Teacheth My Hands to War, To Break My Enemies.
12. Thou Hast Also Given Me The Shield Of Thy Salvation: And Thy Right Hand Hath Holden Me Up;
13. He Has Made Me Great, By His Gentle Hand.
14. As For Stability: Thou Hast Enlarged My Steps Under Me, That My Feet Did Not Slip.
15. Regarding Victory, Ole: I Have Pursued Mine Enemies, and Overtaken Them Neither Did I Turn Again Till They Were Consumed.
16. Assurance And Complete Victory: I Have Wounded Them That They Were N Able to Rise: They Are Fallen Under My Feet.
17. The Future is Bright: Victory is Certain, For Thou Hast Girded Me With Strength for Battle:
18. My Enemies Are No longer a Big Deal, Thou Hast Subdued Under Me Those That Rose Up Against Me.
19. They Will Surrender; Thou Hast Also Given Me the Necks of Mine Enemies; That I Might Destroy Them That Hate Me.
20. Nowhere to Run: They Cried, But There Was None to Save Them: Even Unto The Lord, But He Answered Them Not.
21. Complete Victory, Completes Assignments, Then Did I Beat Them Small as th Dust Before The Wind: I Did Cast Them Out as The Dirt in The Streets.
22. No Weapon Against Me Shall Prosper: Thou Hast Delivered Me From The Strivings of the People; and Thou Hast Made Me The Head of the Heathen:

23. Of My Dominance: A People Whom I Have Not Known Shall Serve Me. As Soon As They Hear of Me, They Shall Obey Me:

24. My Dominance Continues: The Strangers Shall Submit Themselves Unto Me. The Strangers Shall Fade Away, and Be Afraid Out of Their Close Places.

25. A Hymn of A Winner: The Lord Liveth; And Blessed Be My Rock; And Let Th
God Of My Salvation Be Exalted.
It is God That Avengeth Me,
And Subdueth The People Under Me.
He Delivereth Me From Mine Enemies:
Yea, Thou Liftest Me Up Above Those That Rise Up Against Me:
Thou Hast Delivered Me from The Violent Man.
Therefore Will I Give Thanks Unto Thee, O Lord, Among The Heathen,
And Sing Praises Unto Thy Name.
Great Deliverance Giveth He to His King;
And Sheweth Mercy to His Anointed,
To David, And to His Seed For Evermore.

Halala uJehovah. My God Rocks. He's PowerFUL, Classy & **_SUPER_**natural

How do I connect into this supernatural life apostle of God? You may be one of many asking this question already; it is possible if you believe. The key to the supernatural is to have faith in God's word. It is the only anchor, leading to trust and faith that He exists, and you are in line for a supernatural experience. **Heb 11:6.** Accept God as the only source and you will like David sing a song of victory before the fights begins.

- Set your priorities aright;
- Develop them to focus more on God;
- Practice faith living, faith healing, faith supplied living, & faith conquered life.
- You need to see progress as a result of your faith; if no progress, check if your conduct and actions are aligning with your convictions.
- Always remember, the apostolic seed *"havapererwi"* will never run out of ideas.
- Let God see your faith burn on the inside and on the outside; 'faith without works is dead' **Js 2:20.**
- As apostolic people; 'You can' 'We can' with the anointing upon us.

Let us explore some further supernatural deeds in the Holy writ; it is important to always remember that whatever is written in the word of God was written for our benefit, so that through the encouragement of scriptures we might have faith (hope). And faith cometh by hearing the word of God, we will zero on that in the chapter on faith. And in **Joshua 3:4**; Joshua said unto the people, 'sanctify yourselves: for tomorrow the Lord will do wonders among you'. And Joshua spake unto the priests, saying, ''Take up the Ark of the Covenant and pass over before the people. And they took up the Ark of the Covenant, and went before the people''.

The preceding victories cannot be explained apart from the wonder working God's hand. The people of the Way are miracle people. As Joshua garnered those victories, each one of God's children can in the same way experience the miraculous hand of Jehovah in any generation. We need to understand the role of worship in fighting spiritual battles; the priests were asked to go in front carrying the ark because worship brings down God's glory. His glory is His presence and His presence is His power and His power is our victory. Hallelujah.

It is no wonder God call us gods. **Psalms 82:6**, 'I have said, 'Ye are gods; and all of you are children of the most High, don't you believe' We are small gods, children of God have got to have some genes of their father. It's supernatural. However, not to mystify our super-nature; everything bears after its own kind, so God gave birth by the Spirit to gods – you and I. We have God's capacity and resemblance within us. God created by words: and you His child how do you birth those miracles? What are you willing to do to access your miracle? Walk the faith, and act the talk, God will never let you down. Speak forth in faith and it shall be, you are supernatural.

'And in those days Hezekiah became sick and was at the point of death. And Isaiah the prophet the son of Amaz came to him, and said to him, "Thus says the Lord, set your house in order, for you shall surely die, you shall not recover. **Isa 38:2**, Then Hezekiah turned his face to the wall (*forsaking everything, ignoring his fate, in discipline, focusing on God*[10]-my emphasis) and prayed to the Lord, and said, ''Please Lord, remember how I have walked before you in faithfulness and with a whole heart, and have done what is good in your sight. And Hezekiah wept bitterly.

---

[10] My Emphasis

Verse 4: "Then the Word of the Lord came to Isaiah, (the *destiny bringer: everything Isaiah, Isaiah, who are you to think you don't need a man of God in your life – some sobering thoughts here[11])* ''Go and say to Hezekiah, thus says the Lord, the God of your father *(favored in his father's memory[12])* David, I have heard your prayer'' Hallelujah apostolic people! God answers prayer as we can see here) and have seen your tears. ''Behold I will add fifteen years to your life! I will deliver you and this city out of the hand of the king of Assyria, and will defend this city''. If heaven can be turned from a course, what is it that cannot be turned to the advantage of the apostolic seed? Nothing in the universe can resist the rebuff, the rebuke, the block and the repellant by you O' supernatural kid of the Almighty God.

It didn't end there: v7, ''this shall be the sign to you from the Lord, that He will do this thing He has promised; *(we are for Signs and Wonders,* **Isaiah 8:18)** 'Behold I will make the shadow cast by the declining sun on the Dial of Ahaz turn back ten steps. So the sun turned back on the Dial of Ahaz the ten steps by which had declined' What! Oh my God! Here is sheer divination: God's supernatural acts being aided by divinator Ahaz, Yes. It's all spiritual engagements that can only be understood by the spiritually tuned, the carnal mind can't comprehend this. May that level of spiritual revelation be granted to you without a withholding from above from today until the Day of Christ.

Here is God, exercising divination; He can do with power whatever He wants to because He is God. He can use even Cyrus or Nebuchadnezzar to send spiritual messages to his people. Just keep your spirit tuned and you will hear His voice soon enough and discern His acts. It's all by revelation: this is what the Apostle calls the food for the mature. As His children, this limitless power and revelation is available to us by His permissive and perfect will, it's upon us to walk in the supernatural domains beginning by faith, then realization. May God change unending courses just for you: may nature submit to you, and may the weather and climate change just for you! May you be so powerful: not only holy like Hezekiah, but powerful like Isaiah and Ahaz with the power to change destinies, to change courses of nature and fates in Jesus' name!

---

[11] My Emphasis
[12] My Emphasis,

And we have the narrative of Gideon, in Judges 6; God can use the despised things of this world to accomplish great things. He is the creator by the way and can do with power anything that power can do – now that's supernatural.

verse 11-17, *"And there came an angel of the Lord, and sat under an oak which was in Ophrah, that pertained unto Joash the Abiezrite: and his son Gideon threshed wheat by the winepress, to hide it from the Midianites. And the angel of the Lord appeared unto him, and said unto him, The Lord is with thee, thou mighty man of valor. And Gideon said unto him, Oh my Lord, if the Lord be with us, why then is all this befallen us? and where be all his miracles which our fathers told us of, saying, Did not the Lord bring us up from Egypt? but now the Lord hath forsaken us, and delivered us into the hands of the Midianites. And the Lord looked upon him, and said, Go in this thy might, and thou shalt save Israel from the hand of the Midianites: have not I sent thee? And he said unto him, Oh my Lord, wherewith shall I save Israel? behold, my family is poor in Manasseh, and I am the least in my father's house. And the Lord said unto him, Surely I will be with thee, and thou shalt smite the Midianites as one man. And he said unto him, If now I have found grace in thy sight, then shew me a sign that thou talkest with me"*

Gideon was facing a terrible experience, *threshing wheat by the winepress, to hide it from the Midianites.* We all know it is not practical to reverse the two harvest places but because of the heat of the battle, the weak and lowly Gideon had to hide. Secondly he was from the least family along the father's tribes. And now to such a one God says, Arise man of valor? Gideon must have said, there is a mistake somehow my Lord. Gideon was so convinced Israel were finished such that he had along debate with the messenger of heaven. God had to give in to his demands for divination, show me a sign said Gideon. And only a sign could convince him heaven were not making a mistake. God relented and allowed the superstitious guy to have what he preferred.

The rest is history as we see the mighty Gideon preparing a sacrifice, the angel just touches it with the tip of his staff and fire consumed the sacrifice. Still some work he did by night for fear but the work of God was accomplished. He did the long forgotten service, down with the altar of Baal. Joash comes to his defense when the man of the city wanted to avenge for Baal, "let Baal defend himself if he is god'. That's where he got the name Jerruabbal – he who will plead for Baal.

36 "And Gideon said unto God, If thou wilt save Israel by mine hand, as thou hast said, Behold, I will put a fleece of wool in the floor; and if the dew be on the fleece only, and it be dry upon all the earth beside, then shall I know that thou wilt save Israel by mine hand, as thou hast said. And it was so: for he rose up early on the morrow, and thrust the fleece together, and wringed the dew out of the fleece, a bowl full of water. And Gideon said unto God, Let not thine anger be hot against me, and I will speak but this once: let me prove, I pray thee, but this once with the fleece; let it now be dry only upon the fleece, and upon all the ground let there be dew. And God did so that night: for it was dry upon the fleece only, and there was dew on all the ground" KJV

It's supernatural, sometimes it takes some divination, sometimes some superstitious act for God to convince His soldiers of the power; the Class and Supernature inside them. Gideon thumped the Midianites with just a few soldiers after this episode with the divine. From ten thousand warriors God requested three hundred and they did the job of ten thousand satisfactorily and Israel was delivered from Midian. It's supernatural!

Of our Big Brother Jesus, at the Mountain of Transfiguration, God says in **Mathew 3:17**; "This is my beloved Son. I take delight in Him. Listen to Him!' HCSB. This was power acts by God; a demo of the divine order. Jesus had taken Peter, James and John up the mountain - a core group among His disciples that could contain the impending higher level of supernatural experience. Not everyone can get into each of the heavens we know. God can even descend and join the dead with the living in a moment of supernatural fellowship. It was very clear that Elijah and Moses had also joined the fellowship of the greats upon the mountain.

And Peter; being so outspoken burst into the obvious; no sense could come out of a man who had just seen the invisible. When God wills it, we can join with angels and those who have gone before in fellowship but it will have lasting effects on our responsive spiritual natures. I always tell my church that times of fellowship and worship invite the heavens in ways we can never understand: we join with angels and the righteous who have gone before. How does it happen? It's supernatural, only those tuned into it will see it with their spiritual eyes. I have seen angelic hosts many times when I get into deep worship and it started when I was three months old in faith on the mountain of prayer. It is a privilege of the apostolic seed to enter such uncommon realms of spirituality. For, surely nothing is impossible for them that believe.

As theologians, when the dead meet with the living we normally call it divination, and that in a negative sense. An example is the witch at Endo and Saul. The Bible says that Samuel came up, from wherever he was lying at rest and rebuked Saul for bringing him up. There is indeed power in divination: however, it's usually applied for evil by the witches of this world.

But with the Dial of Ahaz, God intended to prove His Omniscient personae, by using an uncommon example to prove a sign for his doubting servant. Witches use divination for various acts of iniquity, and we better watch out because they are the ones against whom we battle in the heavenly realms. The danger is that what we know they also do know, it is our duty to exercise what we know so that we overcome forces of darkness and their agents. Could I be calling you to divination, no, but those whom God grace with it – shine in it. I already practice divination as I use my mouth and even set fire upon my enemies.

I even pronounce miscarriages upon the plans of the devil regarding all that's mine; I declare no witch can touch me or my family without being burnt, I send back any witchcraft to harm the sender. I suffer no witch to live, **Exo 22:18**! That's the level where I am at the present moment, I would ask God for more. I have fought beasts in the spirit, I have received my daughter from death, and I have been delivered from staring the heavens in near death. How could I ask for more, He has done so much for me.

And when the righteous departed, meeting with Jesus and holy saints still alive, that's another level of divination; we are divine and we better start divinating as Holy Spirit leads us. Lest we walk the earth powerless and weak; till the dreadful day wherein we may stumble into glory having been of no effect upon the face of the earth. We must start now to trample down snakes and scorpions and to overcome all the power of the enemy. Jesus gave the license, "And he said unto them, I beheld Satan as lightning fall down from heaven. Behold, I give unto you power to tread on serpents and scorpions, and over all the power of the enemy: and nothing shall by any means hurt you, **Luke 10:18-19.** Your super-nature awaits!

God tells the world of Jesus from the mountain, "Hear Him" and of us He echoes the same sentiments to our foes and opposition. He calls and bellows from heaven to the earth below and the worlds beneath: "This is _____ my beloved son/daughter: - hear him. Are you ready for your supernatural endeavors? God has allowed it. He thunders, "Hear her" to your sickness, your enemies, your friends, earthly problems, the challenges of life; sickness, pain, poverty, the mountains, the speaking trees and stubborn walls. He says, ''Hear him'' May you be too hot to handle for any witch in your earthly walk.

May you be too hot to handle for any sickness or disease! May you be heard when you roar: you are carrying a lion inside you, fear nothing. May you be heard by those valleys, and those mountains, trees, rivers and walls delaying your break-throughs. Act like a god, walk in your Father's shoes; demons tremble, strongholds tumble down before you. You are supernatural when you walk in the Spirit. Hear me friends, we are so powerful: as soon as you open your mouth, they hear, the challenges have been instructed by God "hear him/hear her!

May God show you signs of your inner power: you carry enormous internal power and strength in you: **1 John 4:4**.Greater is He who is in you that ne he who is in the world. You are the elect, chosen and selected by God for special purposes. May you be like an arrow in God's hand, a spear of offense, a game changer, a pacesetter and master-class of the Divine Will. May God change courses just for you; may you be so powerful, not only holy like Hezekiah, but powerful like the divinators of old: Gideon asked for a sign and it was granted. Oh ye! Like Isaiah and Ahaz who were granted the power to change some divine decree regarding the King. For Joshua the sun stood still until he had vanquished his enemies, it sure gets hotter in the spiritual arenas and manifest power on earth.

 May you be like a spiritual legislator, a spiritual Judge, a spiritual Ruler, a god kind of actor in the spiritual places with such power to function in the supernatural. It's yours in Christ and all this I ask for you and on your behalf in the Mighty Name of Jesus Christ. May nothing be impossible to you, for with your God there is no impossibilities. All things are possible.

CHAPTER 5
CLASSICAL FAITH

The great apostle of faith of the nineteenth century shared a deep, thought provoking statement regarding faith. He said, 'Great faith is the product of great fights. Great testimonies are outcome of great tests. Great triumphs can only come out of great trials'. That was Smith Wigglesworth as he nailed what we all know but do not want to hear often. Indeed a testimony cannot be just a line of bliss and bling over one's seventy or ninety year errand on mother earth; there sure must be more.

The legends of biblical heroism went through fire, hell, water, torture and turmoil. Some lost their eyes, yet still others were sawn in two, others were crucified in public as a gesture on the vitrolity of satanic battle against the knowledge of God. The record paints a glim picture of the heroes and heroines who withstood great persecution in order to please their God. We also should walk in their footsteps though in different circumstances. Apostolic people have been called to exude great enthusiasm leading to great faith leading to great tests and great triumphs.

Wigglesworth went on to narrate the spiritual condition of the souls of faithless saints, of whom we should not be party. He shared some painful reality I am challenging you to say, No' to if you would be a victorious apostolic child. He said, "One[13] half of the trouble in the assemblies is the people's murmuring over the conditions they are in. The Bible teaches us not to murmur. If you reach that standard, you will never murmur anymore. You will be above murmuring. You will be in the place where God is the absolute exchanger of thought, the exchanger of actions, and the exchanger of your inward purity.

He will be purifying you all the time and lifting you higher and you will know that you are not of this world" Yes! You are in this world but not of it; that's a mystery of our faith. And Jesus alluded to this in His special prayer for us; "Father, I do not ask that remove them from the world, but that you be with them in this world as you were with me' **John 17.**

People of faith are ordinary people who decide to believe and take God at His word. Apostolic people are so immersed in the word that the word becomes the only source of life; both to the spirit and the material. When eyes are on God, there will be less

---

[13] Smith Wigglesworth Faith Quotes

murmuring in the assemblies, to borrow Wigglesworth's words. The families and homes will palaces of peace and the church becomes a home to the homeless; if only the word would be allowed to rule and dwell richly in our hearts.

Apostolic people manifest daring faith, it is our nature and our DNA, and the agenda is to enforce God's will upon the earth. Faith is not only for the troubled or the suffering, but is our core being as children of God. For indeed without faith it is impossible not only to please God, but even to come to Him. Anyone who comes to Him must believe that He is, and that He is a rewarder to them that diligently seek Him. We have mentioned that this is not blind following, but enlightened worship centered upon conviction and trust.

And what is this faith we are discussing in this section some may ask? Faith according to scripture is the evidence of things not seen, and substance of things hoped for[14]. It comes in varying degrees and sizes as we can conclude from scripture that faith can either be weak or strong, dead or alive, passive or proactive etc. I am proving to you through Scripture that faith is measurable and that it can grow. The Bible talks about growing faith **(2 Thessalonians 1:3)**. And a careful look at **Acts 6:5** says Stephen was full of faith, an implication that there can be empty faith somewhere.

We can go on and on; the Bible is rich with great instructions regarding faith dynamics. **James 2:5** mentions rich faith an implication that some have poor faith. **James 2:22** speaks of a perfect faith implying reality of imperfect faith. **First Timothy 1:5** speaks of unfeigned faith, or faith that is genuine and sincere. **First Timothy 1:19**[15] speaks of shipwrecked faith and of holding on to faith and to a good conscience.

And First John 5:4 speaks of overcoming faith which becomes an anchor to trouble man-soul once enlightenment is received regarding faith that brings victory. I have zeroed more on this subject in my earlier book, "Faith That Conquers" you can get a copy at my market online and even print for yourself from www.amazonkindledirectpublishing/drcardwellnyaungwa[16] bookshelf or simply register as an Amazon customer.

---

[14] Hebrews 11:1 KJV definitions
[15] The English Standard Version online biblia-app
[16] Bookshelf for Dr Cardwell Nyaungwa books on Amazon Marketplaces

Faith must be substantial and effective; God want you strong, dynamic, alive, unyielding, powerful and unbeatable. It must be a burning feel on the inside, a passion springing conviction that does not doubt God's unlimited power. It is a fire, we are a fire people; exhibiting great passions regarding the urgency of our earthly sojourn. We have no day to waste; we live to the fullest and on the edge. This is why He gave us power; to do various acts of heroism in the earth. With the right attitude of faith, We Can; as promised in scripture:

- Trample down snakes and scorpions;
- Overcome all the power of the enemy;
- Suffer no witch to exist;
- Demolish strongholds and punish arguments;
- Scale over the walls and run through troops;
- Go about, doing good, wherever we go, delivering all who are oppressed by the devil;
- Stand on firm foundation: standing our ground in the word.
- Resist the devil and he will run away from us.

I have intentionally left out all the scriptures to the above statements, find them and be like the people of Berea, who after the apostles had finished preaching, they went home and searched the scriptures to see if what was preached was exactly what is written in the Bible. What an apostolic people we see at Berea, such a burning desire to know the truth creates fire on the inside that burns through onto the outside. Such zeal based on deeper and truer knowledge is what the world yearns for.

More on faith, a critical look at Luke 5:18[17] will help us enrich our hearts with more faith insights: ''And behold, men brought in a bed a man which was taken with palsy: and they sought means to bring him in, and to lay him before him. And when they could not find by what way they might bring him in because of the multitude, they went upon the housetop, and let him down through the tiling with his couch into the midst before Jesus''

And when he saw their faith, he said unto him, ''Man, thy sins are forgiven thee''. 'And the scribes and the Pharisees began to reason, saying, ''Who is this which speaketh blasphemies? Who can forgive sins, but God alone?'' But when Jesus

---

[17] KJV is public domain

perceived their thoughts, He answering said unto them, 'Why reason ye in your hearts? Whether is easier, to say, Thy sins be forgiven thee; or to say, Rise up and walk? But that ye may know that the Son of man hath power upon earth to forgive sins, He said unto the sick of the palsy, I say unto thee, Arise, and take up thy couch, and go into thine house'. And immediately he rose up before them, and took up that whereon he lay, and departed to his own house, glorifying God. And they were all amazed, and they glorified God, and were filled with fear, saying, ''we have seen strange things today[18]'' When you find Jesus you have found the miracle.

Apostolic people could have said, "here is power manifest' or declared in loud voices, "we are for signs and wonders'. How low the Pharisees and Sadducees were: the man of faith will do all he can to achieve; faith is a lifestyle, we can do no other. The friends of this sick guy were people of extraordinary faith; we do not hear them asking the owner of the house for permission to remove the roof; it was a moment of the supernatural, and Jesus normally responds is commensurate fashion to such exhibitions of faith. Here is the sum of our interpretation to this faith episode:

> Satan has a short lifespan; Jesus is eternal.
> The man came being carried on a bed;
> The bed was carrying the man, Satan's schemes to discredit your life;
> Faith did not matter what the people were going to say;
> Faith did not stop on the way: hardships don't stop people of faith;
> They navigated the work of the devil with wit and craft,
> They reached the healer Jesus who was amazed at their faith;
> Jesus responds with the miracle of healing;
> Tables are turned at the feet of Jesus.
> The man-carrying bed was carried back home by same man after his faith met healing;
> Jesus can turn the tables for the apostolic generation if we dare believe;
> Our faith is the link to the miraculous.

There is power in the apostolic life, but it only works with the power of your faith in the name of Jesus. Speak boldy to your challenges; speak back to the disease, the pain, the demon in your marriage, the eater in your finances, the sin that easily takes you down all the time, conquer your key moments by faith[19]. Refuse to be ordinary, you are extraordinary. You are the apostolic seed. Turn the tables: the bed which carried the sick must be carried back home by a the healthy being. Tell your money to stop

---

[18] KJV is public domain
[19] OS TAPERA , LEAD INSTITUTE 2009

sneaking away like snakes and remain and increase. Decree daily that 'money cometh', as Gloria Copeland[20] our mother in the faith always teach. That which the devil has stolen must by faith return in the name of Jesus. You are God's elect, chosen to declare His majesty to the universe. Surely as all creation awaits with eager anticipation for the manifestation of the sons of God – will you be left behind while others shine forth in faith and deeds of power. Make your mark and be counted!

Confess who you are each day and believe in the power of positive confession, this is not blind confession, but enlightened declarations of who you are in God. ''Death and life are in the power of the tongue, and they that love it shall eat the fruit **thereof'' Pro 18:21**. The fruit of the tongue is the product of your confessions, your confessions do create a destiny for you. Make the decrees count each morning[21]:

    A. I walk by faith and not by sight, my senses come second to my faith.
    B. I can see the invisible through Holy Spirit's inspiration.
    C. I do not murmur, I bless and give thanks.
    D. I am a woman of virtue through my faith.
    E. My inheritance is victory, my first name is Victory, my surname is Victory.
    F. I am generous for I am amply supplied according to God's riches in glory.
    G. I live an honorable life; I am a child of God.

Therefore I conclude without a shadow of doubt that I doubt the devil, I will never believe his lies. For I am full of faith; my faith is alive, productive, rich, rewarding, growing and conquering in the Mighty Name of Jesus.

---

[20] Gloria and Kenneth are Founders and leaders of Kenneth Copeland Ministries and Eagle Mountain Church
[21] Power Decrees by Dr Cardwell Nyaungwa @COAN GILEAD 2017 SERMONS

CHAPTER 6
A KINGDOM PEOPLE; CLASSICAL LIVING

Apostolic people are a people of the kingdom; they live out Kingdom lives according to Biblical kingdom principles. They are governed and guided by set values that reflect God in their personal and corporate lives. Their king is King Jesus whose domain consists of all creation under Him. ''Therefore God has highly exalted him and bestowed on him the name that is above every name, so that at the name of Jesus every knee should bow, in heaven and on earth and under the earth, and every tongue confess that Jesus Christ is Lord, to the glory of God the Father'' **Phil 2:9-11.**

Apostolic people have a mandate from Him to run His Kingdom on earth, and fashion it as the heavenly kingdom. What a privilege and an honor, to worship at His throne, and to be called into His presence as His own people! It is imperative that apostolic people develop a Kingdom mindset; we have had a lot about Kingdom principles from various writers and we will interest ourselves in this section with the attributes of kingdom people; a people of power and fire, a people of the supernatural kingdom. These are a people of ethics, principles and morals, I dedicated a whole book to discuss ethical living in my short book, 'Ethics Unlimited'. You can get it as also on the Amazon Kindle.

Kingdom people are people whom God the heavenly Father calls His own: they are dear to Him. **Isa 43:1**:

'Now this is what the Lord says - the One who created you, Jacob, and the One who
formed you, Israel — "Do not fear, for I have redeemed you;
I have called you by your name; you are Mine.
I will be with you when you pass through the waters,
and when you pass through the rivers, they will not overwhelm you.
You will not be scorched when you walk through the fire,
and the flame will not burn you.
For I Yahweh your God, the Holy One of Israel, and your Savior, give Egypt as a
ransom for you, Cush and Seba in your place.
Because you are precious in My sight and honored, and I love you, I will give
people in exchange for you and nations instead of your life'
Isa 43:1-7. ESV[22]

Dear to Him and precious in His sight are the people of God. He will go to any length according to the above text in order to make sure it goes well for His people. He offers deliverance, restoration, care and all good things unto his chosen. No good thing will

---

[22] The ESV is public domain

He withhold from them that walk uprightly. **Ps 84:11**. This people will not settle for The average; they have chosen their God and they will honor Him with their very lives. A people He calls His own: they carry an extraordinary spirit, the Spirit that is of God Is their director. He is a spirit of excellence, lifting man to God's standards and expectations.

It becomes an inspiration upon all apostolic people to live up to God's expectations; that's Kingdom living. An excellent creation should be of an excellent disposition: there has to be a difference between those of God, and those not of His Kingdom. Excellence is not a choice but it's who we are. We cannot settle for less, that will be an insult to our God. We represent a greater kingdom that is why the Bible admonishes us to always put our minds on higher things:

Phil 4:8-9[23]

"Finally, brethren, whatsoever things are true; whatsoever things are honest; whatsoever things are just; whatsoever things are pure; whatsoever things are lovely; whatsoever things are of good report; if there be any virtue, and if there be any praise, think of these things. Those things, which ye have both learned, and received, and heard, and seen in me, <u>DO</u>: and the God of peace shall be with you"

We will do a mini commentary on the variables in this text; the List of things to Consider is marvelous and beautiful, isn't it! "Finally, brethren; the Apostle's closing Remarks demands our maximum attention.

➤ He admonishes us to think of these things: if the word of an Apostle carries weight; let's take heed.
➤ What we have taught you, by word or our conduct, do also.
➤ When that command is obeyed and met, the peace of God shall be with you.
➤ We are putting our reputation on the line by assuming you will be our replica in this faith.
➤ This is a list of excellence, there is no variation in Him, so shall it be with us.

WHATSOEVER THINGS THAT ARE;
Let us interest ourselves yet again with a list here, this Holy List will help us breakdown the message on heart of the Apostle Paul. Whatsoever things are;
    (i)   True,
    (ii)   Whatsoever things are Honest,
    (iii)   Whatsoever things are Just,

---

[23] The ESV is public domain

(iv)   Whatsoever things are Pure,
(v)   Whatsoever things are Lovely,
(vi)   Whatsoever things are of Good Report;
(vii)   if there be any Virtue;
(viii)   If there be any Praise, think on these things.

He ends with an apostolic command; 'Those things, which ye Have both learned, and received, and heard, and seen in me, do: and the God of peace shall be with you' Here is the genius of the apostle and his people's Kingdom: remember this is the same man who by the Spirit of God, said, "Follow me as I follow Christ!" It is our responsibility to run God's Kingdom; this is not about a church or a denomination, but a composition of the whole Body of Christ. It is a consolidation of those who by conviction and devotion have agreed to be called an apostolic and prophetic people through the New Birth and training in righteousness.

Jehovah expects each and every group that calls itself by his Name to adhere to the leading of Holy Spirit and the scriptures. However, it's not every church, denomination or believer that shall walk in this supernatural arena: but those who by the Spirit's leading, by true discipleship and revelatory exposition have come to accept their elevated status and position in Christ. Rise up ye apostolic servants of the Most High and exhibit what the world has been yearning for all these years of futility. Indeed those who manifest themselves in this extraordinary fashion will be able to fulfill God's agenda upon their lives; that the whole world may see and acknowledge who are the sons of God. By living out kingdom lives; the saints of God shall take the Kingdom and reign forevermore, it begins with managing the earth as heirs of the divine, nothing else will do.

With a Kingdom mindset, we will stand for God and not the Denomination; there is a time to stand for your denomination when threatened by the enemy of the church. But our primary focus must be to contend for the faith that has once and for all been entrusted to the saints by defending the Kingdom. Heretics speak more of the 'kingdom' than Evangelicals and Bible believing churches yet they don't even know that the key battle is the battle for the kingdom, and not for denominations. Apostolic people must take centre stage in the promotion of the Kingdom of God, we have a lasting Kingdom here, there is nothing to be ashamed or to fear about it. We are creatures of dominion for we belong to the ruling team.

''And this Gospel of the Kingdom shall be preached in the entire world for a witness unto all nations; and then shall the end come'' **(Mathew 24:14)**[24] These are the words of our Lord Jesus Christ in His final ministry days on earth. We will agree that a man's words towards the end of his earthly sojourn carry a special place as guidance or warning to those who remain. It is critical to note that the verse speaks of the 'Gospel of the Kingdom'. What are the implications of this text;

- Apostolic people are called upon to preach the Gospel of the Kingdom.
  - There is an implication here that there a various kinds of gospels.
- We can mention the gospel of man, of prosperity, of suffering; of liberality etc; some imbalanced spiritual doses.

We have made a choice as the CHURCH OF ALL NATIONS & Gilead International Ministries as to which gospel we will preach;

- And it is the Gospel of the Kingdom: That Jesus came, lived, suffered, died, rose, and went back to heaven;
- That Jesus is the answer for the world in any generation;
- No other Gospel come close, even as we know there is no other.

We yearn for the salvation of souls; the deliverance of the bound; the healing of the sick, the liberty of the captives, the demonstration of the power of God, the conviction of authorities and the opening of blind eyes. We long for the salvation of the whole world in our lifetime and are not afraid to spend and be spent for the cause of the Kingdom'' For surely the whole earth shall be filled with the knowledge of the word of the Lord, just as the waters cover the seas. We can take this further with the following scriptures;

Isa 49:5,6

''And now, saith the Lord that formed me from the womb to be his servant,
to bring Jacob again to him,
Though Israel be not gathered,
yet shall I be glorious in the eyes of the Lord,
and my God shall be my strength.
And he said, It is a light thing that thou shouldest be my servant
to raise up the tribes of Jacob,
and to restore the preserved of Israel:
I will also give thee for a light to the Gentiles,
that thou mayest be my salvation unto the end of the earth''

God did not call us to denominations but that through our various churches we can play our part in the business of His Kingdom. It's not even sufficient to Him for someone to

---

[24] ESV online Edition, Olive

be just born again and await entry into heaven: there is more. True it is that we are called to greater impact and influence than the weekly Sunday service; that not being bad in its own it has actually been ordained to be an equipping tool for people to go out and make a difference in their communities, their nations and the world at large.

The church as we call it becomes a place for ministry training; the real ministry is outside the walls of church building as people exhibit their faith to the saving of the lost. And God wishes that more of us will go to the ends of the earth, to the un-churched and unreached. He wishes us go out and carry the flame of truth to every Hindu, every Muslim and Animist across the globe. They are like the Biblical Macedonian call; the 10/40 Window is calling, the Middle East and North Africa Muslim-infested lands and the lost tribes of the Asian Continent are yearning for a new approach from the people of the Kingdom of God.

And at present the First World is backsliding rapidly; I have personally seen church buildings cracking and falling in Holland, Switzerland, Belgium etc due to disuse. Closer home in Kempton Park we have had three traditional Pentecostal Churches buildings lie idle for a couple of years only for two to be revived by a new renting church and the other by a gym. The third assembly is still dead as we write. This is not ideal; the church needs a kingdom people to reach out to these lands and proclaim the Gospel of the Kingdom. This is Kingdom business in as much as preaching on Sunday, as building an auditorium or administration as full time workers in the church office is. Let us carry the Kingdom burden and our denominational burdens become lighter.

Psalms 2:7-12
''Ask of me, and I shall give thee the heathen for thine inheritance,
and the uttermost parts of the earth for thy possession.
Thou shalt break them with a rod of iron;
thou shalt dash them in pieces like a potter's vessel.
Be wise now therefore, O ye kings:
be instructed, ye judges of the earth.
Serve the Lord with fear, and rejoice with trembling.
Kiss the Son, lest he be angry,
and ye perish from the way,
when his wrath is kindled but a little.
Blessed are all they that put their trust in him''

'Ask of me and I will give you' it is God's call to place the burden of salvation on our hands because we are the ambassadors of His Kingdom on earth. He promised to give us success if we obey to do evangelism. The word says, ''ask of me and I will give you''. The heart of the matter becomes the nations and their peoples: 'Heathens for your inheritance, and the ends of the earth (nations) for your possession'. This is God's heart and it sure must be the passion of every apostolic seed – to win souls. Depopulating hell and filling heaven is a fulfilling assignment. What a joy it shall be on that great day! What would stop us as apostolic people from soul winning and witnessing seeing God has opened the door for success in that department?! What excuse would we give for not evangelizing?

Prophet Ezekiel caps it all with an astonishing implication, ''If I say to the wicked person, ''You will surely die, but you do not warn him — you don't speak out to warn him about his wicked ways in order to save his life — that wicked person will die for his iniquity. Yet I will hold you responsible for his blood. But if you warn a wicked person and he does not turn from his wickedness or his wicked way, he will die for his iniquity, but you will have saved your life'' Move over to the Kingdom and reach out, teach, touch, bless and heal the nations with the power of God in you. It's an assignment that we must carry out without fail. God entrusted the population of heaven into our hands. We have no excuse but to stand up for the Kingdom. There are consequences to disobeying the order, the blood of the sinner who would rather have heard the gospel from you will be accounted at your hands.

Let us undo the divisions in the churches and declare ourselves a people of God and a people of Christ. Let us join hands in the heartbeat of evangelism, all other areas will go just fine if we do well in aligning the Kingdom mindset upon the elect. A Kingdom divided against itself cannot stand. United we can march against the forces of Satan and claim every possible soul and channel it on the way to eternal life in Christ. Let us embrace the Kingdom principle and see God act out His way and hasten the return of Christ. Kingdom people rule the earth with an eye on heaven, that's who we are. Come Lord Jesus.

Confession of a Kingdom People

1. Lord, deliver me from sins of commission;
2. Deliver me from sins of omission (disobedience);
3. Deliver me from mediocrity; loving junk. I am not junk, I am class; devil hear me. I am a jewel.
4. Deliver me from avoiding excellence with lame excuses.
5. Deliver me from withholding that which I must give.
6. Deliver me from withholding that which carries my miracle and should be sacrificed
7. Deliver me from self, I am a hindrance to my excellent living as a Kingdom Prince.
8. Deliver me from the sin of my fathers, the sin of my mothers, the sin of my ancestors that is holding me back from an experiencing Kingdom Dominion.

9. I break loose from any bondage; either demonic or denominational, spiritual or physical, financial or relational, I break loose in Jesus Mighty Name!
10. Deliver me from friends and associations that are used by the devil to hold back my growth, success and prosperity.
11. Deliver me from friends and associations that are used by the devil to hold back my Kingdom Impact and Influence.
12. Deliver me Lord I am ready for my freedom to be an excellent participant in your Kingdom.
13. Deliver me from living a life below your standard for which you died for me on the cross;
14. Deliver me from disobeying your word through not sacrificing;
15. Deliver me from disobeying your word through Not Tithing;
16. Deliver me from disobeying your word through not praying always as scripture encourages me.
17. I am embracing Kingdom mentality beginning now till the Lord returns.
18. Thy Kingdom Come, Thy will be done in my life as it is in heaven.
19; Deliver me Lord:
   - I Am Moving into Apostolic and Prophetic Living;
   - I am a Kingdom Prince/ss,
   - Deliver me from fear: then your Power and the Glory are mine in Jesus' name.
   - Deliver me so that I start to reflect the nature of my father's house;
   - Deliver me from these chains; visible of invisible, known or unknown – deliver me Lord.
   - Deliver me and use me Lord for the saving of souls.
   - Deliver me that I start today to be a blessing: a blessing at home, in my marriage, at work, in my church – make me a blessing Lord. Deliver me and anoint me!
   - I am going out there to walk in apostolic and prophetic power.

I am renewed, I am revived, I am anointed! I have overcome with my kingdom status in Jesus' Name and I pray right now:

'Our Father who art in heaven, Hallowed be thy name. Thy Kingdom come. Thy will be done in earth, as it is in heaven. Give us this day our daily bread. And forgive us our sins, as we forgive those who sin against us. And lead us not into temptation, but deliver us from evil: For thine is the Kingdom, and the power, and the glory, forever and ever' Amen

CHAPTER 7

THE DOMINION FUNCTUM
'Power Manifests'

There are mysteries that the Bible presents to us that are difficult to interpret especially from prophetic books. One of them is the book of Ezekiel, a book I normally call "The Book of Priesthood' but far be it from us to assume it is about priests only. We will try in this section to link the original purpose why man was created and the mysteries of Ezekiel. Bible teachers have an obligation to the cross to explain such mysteries to the world.

Throughout the ages there have been types and symbols used by God and by man in explaining or interpreting each other, in a framework that seeks to reveal to us the Kingdom Functum and enhance the covenant. We have explained the Kingdom in previous chapters, that it's a domain run by a King and his subjects. Apostolic people are vassals and subjects in that domain. We can safely agree with Pastor Lameck Sinoia of Dunamis Faith Centre in Swansea, Wales when he says, ''a classic definition of a kingdom is a territory subject to the rule of a king. But there is another definition equally as operative in the Greek language for the word *Basilela* referring to the kingdom of heaven according to the Bible[25].

It is a royal power, a kingship and dominion not to be confused with earthly kingdoms, but rather the right and authority to rule over a kingdom. In other words, a kingdom isn't necessarily a tract of land or a collection of cities however these may form part or components to a domain. So God's kingdom is universal, never think lightly of those who call themselves a people of the Kingdom, there is power and authority vested in them. This kingdom is spiritual, the carnal mind cannot comprehend it, this is clearly stated in **1 Cor 2:14**, it's spiritually discerned. It is beyond common sense faculties to understand.

Now let us get back to the book of priesthood as we reveal the kingdom functum with apostolic people depicted as components of the same. Ezekiel saw so many visions that the whole book is like a movie. We will interest ourselves with only one such from Ezekiel Chapter One for the purpose of this book. This vision signifies the significance of man's service as a vassal of the Great King. **Ezekiel 1:10** speaks of an appearance by the four faced living creatures. The imagery is signifying the creatures' mobility and functions as they attend the throne of the heavenly King who is ever on the move according to this book and the book of Revelations and we are using KJV language specifics to this conclusion. As man attends the Kingdom of God here on earth where he is ordained to rule and reign; these four faces paint a very important picture on the

---

[25] Lameck Sinoia mobile Morning Devotionals, 2017

essence of the anointing for God's service. The specific graces that empower man to rule are typically the faces that Ezekiel saw. We will spend the next paragraphs trying to simplify and explain as well as interpret the functums represented thereby. This applies as man serves as priest and king (in apostolic grace) running the Kingdom of the Great King above.

The prophet Ezekiel gives us four pictures or faces: Lion, Man, Ox and Eagle. First is the lion; apart from the lion depicting the Lion of the Tribe of Judah, we have here man, represented as a (ruler) a vassal of God's kingdom. Our kingdom function demands our strongest nature; for our warfare both natural and spiritual demands the heart of a lion. The Apostle Paul says we face a mighty battle against the forces of evil, calling upon our very best battleground personae. He says to put on our full armor for the battle is huge, **Eph 6:10.**

And the lion was the most ferocious beast of the wild known in Israel and Mesopotamia, and reputedly the strongest of all beasts, this is attested everywhere you go. Like lions; God also wants His vassals strong in faith, undefeated, defiant and dominant. The man of God must take charge just as the lion rules and dominates the jungle. For God has not given us the spirit of fear, but the spirit of power, of sound mind and sober judgment, **1 Tim 2:7.** Therein lie the call to the lion heart, the lion face and the lion spirit if we are to manifest the dominion functum.

Next Ezekiel gives us the face of a man as it unraveled in his vision. Man is the most celebrated creatures on earth and in heaven. God did not give man dominion only, but endowed him with God's own likeness – taken it whichever way we may, it's no small deal to be made in the image of God. We will come back deeper to this later on. God's image became like a signet ring on man's finger from the creator; it is all authority to manage the kingdom on God's behalf. Only heaven and hell has man no power to manage, but he can influence what happens in both pieces of the domain by evangelism and soul winning; Yes, the population of hell and heaven is dependent upon man. It is one of the mysteries.

We define man also as a creature of beauty; that is why among all creation, only man is capable of dressing, capable of make-up and capable of the faculties of beauty and intelligence. A little lower than the angels, man has been crowned with God's self: the very attributes of the Lord can be very visible in a saved soul. They can make or break man's destiny. Man is the only creature upon which after creation God said to His council, very good! Halleluiah!
Man is the only creature unto whom God vested authority and social responsibility: it's no mean an assignment. The power of judgment has been placed on man by God. With

words man has capacity to pronounce and make impacting decrees: "Death and life are in the power of the tongue: and they that love it shall eat the fruit thereof" **Pro 18:21.** This is a kingly aspect whereby the word of the king has authority and effect upon destinies. The priestly functum also becomes a serious matter once we understand that in man is *duality*: there is God and there is man.

The Ezekiel faces of 'Ox and Eagle cap a very enriching theological narrative: a blessing and inspiration to those who are of the kingdom. The ox is the most powerful of all domesticated animals. It speaks of labor, hard work, production, fruitfulness, profit, value and friendliness. It is more important to the household than any farm animal thus our importance exceeds that of all creation in God's domain. It behoves upon us that we tame the cobras and the vipers, that we ride the lions to work and eat the best fish of the deep seas. All creation await with eager anticipation for our manifestation of this order.

The eagle has always been painted as an elevated animal above all birds, but that's not all there is to the eagle. The heights are a strategy to deal with the deeps. It is the mightiest of the birds. Its face being ascribed unto man is all about perception, vision, revelation, elevation and focus. The eagle can kill any kind of snake: like us we have in us inherent divine enablement to kill any kind of demon. We are elevated in the anointing. God expects us to keep our minds on the things above, yet still we dominate the earth below.

We now get to the origins of the dominion functum of man; it was granted immediately upon creation, not as an after-thought on God's part.

Gen 1:26-28

26; "And God said, Let us make man in our image, after our likeness: and let them have dominion over the fish of the sea, and over the fowl of the air, and over the cattle, and over all the earth, and over every creeping thing that creepeth upon the earth.

27; So God created man in his own image, in the image of God created he him; male and female created he them.

28; And God blessed them, and God said unto them, Be fruitful, and multiply, and replenish the earth, and subdue it: and have dominion over the fish of the sea, and over the fowl

of the air, and over every living thing that moveth upon the earth" In the original languages, at the end of every act of creation the Bible said God so that it was good, but when it came to man, the remarks develops to and He saw that it was very good.

- The creation of man was very good, so something very good must come out of him.

- The Great I Am says I am, present tense, so His decrees last the eternities, therefore man you are still very good.

- 'Behold He has made everything beautiful in its time, and He has placed eternity in the hearts of man' **Ecc 3:11**. Man's dominion will last and he shall reign even with Christ after the end of the age.

- Some theological teachers call Him *"The God of the Now" He has no past tense.* **Heb 13:8** says, ''Jesus Christ the same yesterday, and today, and forever''. So, what He made centuries ago and decreed stands forever.

What God said to man in Genesis is settled forever: man can trust God to allow him to reign in an unending Kingdom. *Oh unchanging God!* ''For I am the Lord, I change not; therefore ye sons of Jacob are not consumed'' **Mal 3:6**. Let's develop this; the appointment of man to manage the earth is a primary call; right at the beginning God ordained him to be the ruler and manger of His interests, He left nothing out of man's grasp. Man is the zenith of God's creation, no other creature will last eternity but man. *Gen 1:29:* ''And God said, Behold, I have given you every herb bearing seed, which is upon the face of all the earth, and every tree, in the which is the fruit of a tree yielding seed; to you it shall be for meat''- and it was so.

Gen 1:30: ''And to every beast of the earth, and to every fowl of the air, and to everything that creepeth upon the earth, wherein there is life, I have given every green herb for meat'' And It Was So! The motto and it was so creates a vital Implication; with
it certainty is confirmed. What does it mean to a twenty first century Christian that all God decreed at creation was so! Does it still hold current in today's world? God does not lie neither changeth He, so even today it is so. This empowerment is suffix to the whole act of creation.

What is it that the Bible alludes to that and 'it was so', and we prophetically confirm that it is so? Let us do a run-down of quick thoughts that come to mind from deducing given texts;

(i) Let us make man in our image – *And it was so;*
(ii) After our likeness – ***Psalms 82:6.***
(iii) Let them have dominion over the fish of the sea; *and it was so.*

(iv)   Over the fowl of the air – *And it was so.*
(v)   And over the cattle *–And it is so.*
(vi)   Over all the earth – *And it is so.*
(vii)   Over every creeping thing that creepeth upon the earth.
(viii)   And God blessed them; Be fruitful, and multiply, and replenish the earth; And subdue it;
(ix)   Have dominion over the fish of the sea;
(x)   Over every living thing that moveth upon the earth;
(xi)   And God blessed them – And it was so;
(xii)   Be fruitful, multiply and replenish the earth – *and it was so- scripture repetition not ours!*
(xiii)   Subdue it – *and it was so.*

''I have given you every herb bearing seed, which is upon the face of all the earth, and every tree, in the which is the fruit of a tree yielding seed; to you it shall be for meat'' *and it is so.*

And man in apostolic grace answereth the Lord, *It is so my Lord;* every word and decree that came from the mouth of the Lord is a 'Yes and Amen' in Christ Jesus. *Let the* only creature with authority rule and reign. Let this dominion function be taken seriously by all God loving souls. Our social responsibility is a mandate; we have no choice by to judge the world in righteousness and our God given authority. Let us walk in it, confess it and make decrees.

Psalms 8

''O Lord our Lord, how excellent is thy name in all the earth!
who hast set thy glory above the heavens.
Out of the mouth of babes and sucklings hast thou ordained strength because of thine enemies,
that thou mightest still the enemy and the avenger.
When I consider thy heavens, the work of thy fingers,
the moon and the stars, which thou hast ordained;
What is man, that thou art mindful of him?
and the son of man, that thou visitest him?
For thou hast made him a little lower than the angels,
and hast crowned him with glory and honour.
Thou madest him to have dominion over the works of thy hands; thou hast put all things under his feet:
All sheep and oxen, yea, and the beasts of the field;
The fowl of the air, and the fish of the sea,

and whatsoever passeth through the paths of the seas.
O Lord our Lord how excellent is thy name in all the earth''

There is nothing smallful about our God, neither should there be anything small about you, we are great in Him. Smallness will not save the world; it's the big guys who do both big and small deeds that bring change and betterment to our world. What are you waiting for. The world and its rulers recognizes you that is why they are always at war with you, you are not in the wrong place; you are rightly placed and God will not allow anything beyond your power allocation to come near you. You and I have the dominion at our disposal so let us rule and exercise authority both in the physical and spiritual realms to the glory of our God. *Dominion*

CHAPTER 8
A PEOPLE OF CHRISTMAS

Apostolic people are a people of Christmas; they are a Christ-inspired people. Nothing earthly can add value to us, but the gift of God – Jesus. We are a Jesus people if we may say. He created us for His own pleasure. He gave Adam the harp above all creation and said, "here, above all creation I want you to worship and praise me more". Unfortunately Adam threw the harp away at the garden temptation. The mantle to rule the garden and all creation was lost when he gave in to the tempter. The fellowship with God was lost and both he and his wife were banished from the presence of God. That was the beginning of trouble for mankind.

However God who is rich in mercy decided to give man chance after chance in each generation. How could He not? After all man is His choice creation; the climax and the zenith of his handiwork. That is the reason why His hand has been extended to man over the centuries. Man has had a bad habit of emotional response without conviction; the patriarchs and prophets failed to restore man back to original purpose in God because of man's stubbornness. But the ultimate, Christmas came to Restore that Covenant lost at Eden. And by Christmas we mean the advent of Christ, and of covenant we do refer to the original union between man and God. Apostolic people have accepted Christmas because they know their God is a covenant keeping God, He wouldn't banish man from His presence forever. He loves His choice creature and friend:
- He agreed with Noah regarding never to destroy the earth with waters again and they set a rainbow as the symbol of their covenant,
- He called Abraham friend;
- He agreed with Moses regarding the Canaan reentry and it was fulfilled.
- He agreed with Abraham and today multitudes shall belong to Abraham's bowels as descendants in the faith.
- He also agreed with the prophets and patriarchs and fulfilled His side of the agreement.

Therefore as a 'covenant keeping God', He has no choice but to fulfill His promises to his people. He fully met His part once and for all when Christ came as a fulfillment to Isaiah's prophecy of the virgin birth. **Isa 1:9**. God does not and will never flip flop on crucial issues. He is God and not a man that He should lie neither is He the son of man that He should change His mind. Only man changes, but not God.

What is my part then in Christmas as an apostolic and prophetic seed? I am made for God's pleasure therefore I must bring joy to Him through my:

- Praising Him for who He is.
- Worship; as the ultimate.
- Sacrifices; He is worthy all.
- Celebration of Life; to confirm the joy of the Lord.
- Adoration; He is our all as apostolic people.

God must say, "aha' whenever I open my mouth to give Him glory. I must with complete confidence and surrender give up all that I am to Him without any reservation. He is my all: I am all His. When Christmas season comes, apostolic people are tuned and alert to the reason for the season. God through Jesus makes us a people of Christmas, we are His and it's all about Him.

- Be careful of the demon of retailers & traders who nullify the essence of the season with their marketing gimmicks.
- Christmas has nothing to do with shopping.
- There is no Christ in shopping unless you are buying gifts to give out.
- Nothing wrong in shopping; but the demon of commerce has taken over Christmas from us, it becomes a problem when shopping tries to be the reason for the season.
- Always remember: money or not, shopping or not, travelling or not, the ''Reason for the Season is Christ''.

The Actual Date
Indeed the dates may not be accurate; what can be accurate about those ancient historical periods' data? But thanks be to God, we at least have some records available preserved by Holy Spirit; the canon stands the test. We don't care its December or June, our Savior was born! Hallelujah! Some of us are using wrong birth dates because of the effects of war; some because our parents forgot or made mistakes.

> Truth Triumphs over Fact#
> Mercy Triumphs over judgment#
> The Spiritual Rules over Fact#

Some definitions: CHRISTMAS in ENGLISH;

CHRIST -	*MASS*
(i)Jesus Christ	(i) Celebrating
(ii) Anointed one	(ii) Gathering
	(iii) Accepting

CHRISTMAS in GREEK
CHRISTos - *M'AZA Kneaded dour/cake*

60

(i) God's Anointed one	(i) Celebrating
(ii) God's Set Apart	(ii) Gathering
	(iii)Accepting

CHRISTMAS in HEBREW

MASSIA - ***MAS Matza, Alleluia***

(i)Ma^–siah	(i) Celebrating
(ii) Messiah	(ii) Gathering
(iii) Savior	(iii) Accepting

'Merry Christmas': these words sound too familiar, but I wonder how many of us know the spiritual meaning behind these two words. Taken at the flood it's a call to celebration yes, and it's also a wish for good memories to be created in the season. But for the apostolic people it has some deeper connotations. Here is spiritual celebration of Christmas;

PSALMS 148:1-5 – Say HALLELUAH and, GIVE THANKS!
''Praise ye the Lord. Praise ye the Lord from the heavens:
praise him in the heights. Praise ye him, all his angels:
praise ye him, all his hosts. Praise ye him, sun and moon: praise him, all ye stars
of light.
Praise him, ye heavens of heavens,
and ye waters that be above the heavens.
Let them praise the name of the Lord:
for he commanded, and they were created''

King David is famous for the last verse of his psalms, **Psalms 150:6**, that calls everything that has breath to praise the Lord. Here He agrees with Christmas: everything in all creation must bow before the King. The moon, the sun and the stars must pay homage to the God of our salvation. The waters below and the heavens above must acknowledge that he is worthy of all praise.

Give thanks with a grateful heart for his creative works. This aligns with **Romans 8:19** that all creation are awaiting with eager anticipation for the manifestation of the sons of God. As human beings, we lead the way, we are the zenith, we are the worshippers. All creation must learn from us what is means to worship; to praise, to adore and to make a joyful noise unto the Lord. At Christmas, may we give thanks to the Lord for his goodness, and let all creation confirm and nod in agreement for He is the reason for the occasion.

The Reason for The Season

Jesus' birth did not happen in private; there was publicity all over Israel regarding the news of the birth of the long awaited Messiah. God could not have the incarnation of His Son be a private affair, it was the heavy sound of Christmas that the world had longed to see. It was also befitting that His crucifixion was also not done in a corner, but publicly for a witness and a testimony of these things. We will give you below some scriptures on Christmas.

Isa 9:1-3: ''Nevertheless the dimness shall not be such as was in her vexation, when at the first he lightly afflicted the land of Zebulun and the land of Naphtali, and afterward did more grievously afflict her by the way of the sea, beyond Jordan, in Galilee of the nations. The people that walked in darkness have seen a great light: they that dwell in the land of the shadow of death, upon them hath the light shined. Thou hast multiplied the nation, and not increased the joy: they joy before thee according to the joy in harvest, and as men rejoice when they divide the spoil'' Jesus came as that Great Light the world had yearned for he became the redemption of man from darkness. Those who walked in affliction find healing in Him. No one else could do the work that he wrought upon the cross of Calvary.

Luke 2:8-14: ''And there were in the same country shepherds abiding in the field, keeping watch over their flock by night. And, lo, the angel of the Lord came upon them, and the glory of the Lord shone round about them: and they were sore afraid. And the angel said unto them, Fear not: for, behold, I bring you good tidings of great joy, which shall be to all people. For unto you is born this day in the city of David a Savior, which is Christ the Lord. And this shall be a sign unto you; 'Ye shall find the babe wrapped in swaddling clothes, lying in a manger. And suddenly there was with the angel a multitude of the heavenly host praising God, and saying,

Glory to God in the highest,
and on earth peace,
good will toward men''

What an epic visitation that was; and what joy with the divine set up; angels and the heavenly host celebrated the fact that Christ had in victory descended to resolve the issue of the covenant once and for all. That's the sweet sound of Christmas, our source of power and evidence of the divine inter-disposition.

Mat 2:1-4: ''Now when Jesus was born in Bethlehem of Judaea in the days of Herod the king, behold, there came wise men from the east to Jerusalem, Saying, Where is he that is born King of the Jews? For we have seen his star in the east, and are come to worship him. When Herod the king had heard these things, he was troubled, and all Jerusalem with him. And when he had gathered all the chief priests and scribes of the people together, he demanded of them where Christ should be born''

He came to shake the power brokers and Herod was not exempt, the fiery countenance on his face was a sign that it was time up that the real Kingdom take over dominion. He had to call for the Royal Council to discuss this issue of a king born outside the king's palace. It was a moment when God was sending a message to the world that He rules by his Son. And David calls upon all, "Kiss the Son, lest he be angry, and ye perish from the way, when his wrath is kindled but a little. Blessed are all they that put their trust in him''

John 3:14-17: ''And as Moses lifted up the serpent in the wilderness, even so must the Son of man be lifted up: That whosoever believeth in him should not perish, but have eternal life. For God so loved the world, that he gave his only begotten Son, that whosoever believeth in him should not perish, but have everlasting life. For God sent not his Son into the world to condemn the world; but that the world through him might be saved'' Christ came as God's gift to the world; the perfect propitiation for our sins. With no price to pay, and no ransom demanded, Jesus became the ransom that brought our freedom to set us free. His death as shameful as it was (see next text) was the perfect as God designed it, that in weakness and pain he may redeem man back to Himself.
There was chastisement, there was mockery, there were wounds, and affliction upon the sinless Christ, that today we can say with joy 'Merry Christmas' He is the reason for the season. **Gal 3:13-14:** ''Christ hath redeemed us from the curse of the law, being made a curse for us: for it is written, Cursed is every one that hangeth on a tree: That the blessing of Abraham might come on the Gentiles through Jesus Christ; that we might receive the promise of the Spirit through faith''

He is The Reason for The Season, 'the Heavy Sound of Christmas'
Luke 4:18: "The Spirit of the Lord is upon me, because He has anointed me to proclaim good news to the poor. He has sent me to proclaim liberty to the captives and recovering of sight to the blind, to set at liberty those who are oppressed, to proclaim the year of the Lord's favor." This was prophesied by Isaiah and Jesus echoed the fulfillment in Him. This has been bestowed upon the apostolic people as a heritage in the faith. The Spirit of the Lord is upon us, making us a cut above the rest, in a class of our own.

The Spirit of the Lord is upon Me, because Has Anointed Me:

63

1. To Proclaim Good News to the Poor;
2. He Sent Me to Proclaim Liberty to the Captives;
3. And Recovering of Sight to the Blind,
4. To Set at Liberty those Who are Oppressed,
5. To Proclaim the Year of The Lord's Favor"

This is our story, our anchor: Christmas is our lifeblood. How we long to be like Him. This is why we cry: Oh, ''How God anointed Jesus of Nazareth with the Holy Ghost and with power, how He Went about doing good wherever He went, delivering all who Were oppressed by the devil, for God was with Him'' **Acts 10:38**. Those who know me well, know how much this verse means to me and my church. It is our desire that Christmas will be given back to the man of Galilee, the man of Christmas.

I am moved to share with you a little bit of some acts of Christmas. It was in the villages of Gennesaret when the Christmas of **Luke 4:18** was fulfilled. Here was legion, a man in whose soul dwelt six thousand different demons. He made his abode among the dead – the tombs were his beds. And on comes Christmas (Christ) on a rare visit to this village. Living among the tombs also meant literally that Legion was dead: possessed by six thousand demons, and living with ghosts there is no worse state to a life than such demonic oppression.

Jesus arrives on the scene, and we can say that day was a Christmas day to sorry Legion. A verbal confrontation ensued, but as usual Christmas won. Legion was a soul for whom Christ had came to earth; demons in him were unwanted foreigners. Jesus is anointed to deliver all who are oppressed by the devil and this man was a candidate. Demons were cast in their thousands and cast into the sea via the swine herd and the man Legion now clean as God originated him sat aside Jesus. Those who knew him could not believe that a man who required dozens of the village men to tie down with chains and fetters but still broke them was now sitting next to a foreigner and chatting normally. Nothing beats Christmas on once tormented a soul. If troubled by demonic spirits, may your Christmas come in such fashion right now in the Name of Jesus. Hallelujah.

And this woman being of Greek origin, of Syrophoenician descent, is among the throngs pressing to meet Jesus. The Lord is ministering as usual and she is there with her twelve year old problem; a bleeding un-ceassant. She had for a long twelve years been in pain and embarrassed because it is supposed to be just a periodic and natural menstrual experience. Not with her; it had become a curse and a chronic struggle. It could have been she had since stopped socializing because no one can stand the anguish of such a life publicly; bleeding of the woman alienates.

Now she knows Jesus is the healer; and she perceives in her heart and got a sure conviction; if only I can touch the hem of His garment, I will be healed. What faith – such, Christmas does not ignore. And the moment she touched the hem of Jesus' garment her bleeding stopped. Her healing quickly appeared in that instant, talk of Christmas in June. This is the power of Christmas, it is not a day, date or month, but its Christ. God anointed Jesus such that He delivers all who encounter Him. Christmas people, apostolic people, power is yours as Jesus has decided to share with you in the anointing of Christmas.

Apostolic people know this that we are a people of Christmas. We wish you a 'Merry Christmas' whether in June, July, August, September, October or January, let every minute be Christmas unto you as you walk the apostolic and prophetic life. Daily we wish you a Merry Christmas. Let miracles happen without an end as you carry the one greater inside you. Even as you read this book, receive your miracle, Christmas is here, in the Name of Jesus. And your part is to agree, Hallelujah Christmas everyday is my portion in Jesus' name.

CHAPTER 9
DYNAMICS OF AN APOSTOLIC PEOPLE 1
'The Acts Model'

The best model we have to describe the apostolic people is the 'Acts Model, there we see the people of God acting out Apostolic faith in the early church. We meet people sold out to The Gospel of the Apostles; and attending to it with their all; holy awe, zeal, passion and total devotion. They lived and created what we today know as the 'Acts of the Apostles' what a befitting name. They had dynamic faith in the Word of God and trusted their apostles' ministry.

This people had a vivid conviction as regards their faith; their souls were sold out to Christ. They had the word or nothing. They were so devoted to the Kingdom of God such that they turned the then known world upside down in partnership with their apostles. They committed themselves to the gospel such that their commitment to the Lord led them to deny themselves and focus on corporate faith: the unity brought the First Revival of **Acts 2:1**[26] and the subsequent miracles were a result of the power of corporate worship. Everything about them was so vivid and dynamic, creating these chapters of the dynamics of an apostolic people.

The Bible records that many signs and wonders were done by the apostles among them. The Acts report reveal that they devoted themselves to the apostles' teachings; their daily assembling in selected homes to hear the message of Jesus is a commendable spiritual feat. The ministry of the early apostles which zeroed on the Risen Christ should be the thrust of the apostles' and prophets' doctrine in any generation. The apostles' zeal and burning desire to evangelize met with commensurate desire of the seekers both from former Judaizers and Gentiles set their world on fire. We can also set our world on fire, not only by doing the right things, but going beyond the ordinary service of ministry.

'They gave themselves first to God, then to the Apostles in accordance with God's will'' **2 Cor 8**. It is God's plan that people give themselves to Christ first, and also to their spiritual leaders so that the equation of the flow of anointing can be complete. There are critics today who because of a few corrupt spiritual leaders, they have decided to nullify the spiritual order; it will not suffice, God has set man to attend the affairs of many, even in the NT that is why Jesus had only twelve apostles in all the world.

---

[26] Acts 2:1 the Outpouring of Holy Spirit

A look at Psalms 133 will help us understand and appreciate this beautiful point of spiritual order: the scriptures tell the story of levels in anointing, levels in measure of grace and levels in any spiritual set up, we have a choice to make.

> *''Behold, how good and how pleasant it is*
> *for brethren to dwell together in unity!*
> *It is like the precious ointment upon the head, that ran down upon the beard,*
> *even Aaron's beard: that went down to the skirts of his garments;*
> *As the dew of Hermon, and as the dew that descended upon the mountains of*
> *Zion: for there the Lord commanded the blessing''* **Ps 133. HSCB**

Here is an admonition and call to order: God admonishes the saints to dwell in unity. In **Acts 2**, Holy Spirit descended when they were in one place and in one accord – that's complete unity. The purpose of having anointed genuine leadership or spiritual superior over you is such that the anointing can flow as God planned it: from the head of Aaron down to the body of believers. Everywhere in the Bible we see the role of the main leader clearly marked by specific grace, and that grace should cascade to every member of the ministry or church. This is the will of God for apostolic people and once its aligned He will come to the party.

Any contrary arrangement is foreign to the Bible, no man should worship and run God's work in solitude, there has to be ordained leadership and no man should ever ordain themselves – that is a heretic act: originating from such self serving acts are false prophets and apostles. It is Biblical for saints to rally behind their leader with a compelling vision; be they either Charismatic or Pentecostal or Evangelical like me. As long as they are led by the Spirit and they are obeying the scriptures, rally behind them and defend their dream, it is God's will for the unity of the church. Do not defend error or heresy because of some advantage you get or follow blindly. Test the spirits even on your leader when he or she goes wrong. Abhor every appearance of evil and cling on to what is right.

'The Acts Report' is very clear: they were together, with one accord, typifying the harmony of musical cords. I play the musical keyboard a little and have a little understanding on the importance of harmony among the keys, the voice, transpose, the tempo and everything at one go. The music becomes music only when there is that harmony. It is the same with the church of God, everything must be done in harmony, even in disagreements there has to be an understanding that we are managing the Holy Thing.

Together is the watchword for a Spirit led church. Walking in faith and loving one another, is a sign that God is present among a people. We exhort all apostolic and prophet churches to bring God's people together, and not divide them – it is Satan's agenda to divide. When divided the church becomes weak and the devil knows that very well and Jesus said a Kingdom divided against itself cannot stand. Let the apostolic people worship in unity and see the glory that carries power manifest among them.

The apostle has a role to play in teaching the church and its leaders in the ways of Jehovah, in as much as the Hebrew child was trained in the Laws of God. There is a fundamental call to act out our faith just as the scripture teaches us; let us walk in the fear of God and the world will acknowledge. We will develop the dynamic to never give up nor surrender; riding on spirit-led patience and persistence. Apostolic people are patriotic and lasting: they know that only God, the souls of saints and His word are eternal, and that all else shall pass away. They stick around the vision long enough to see its fulfillment.

We are talking about born again and spirit filled saints who shall reign with Christ both now and in eternity. They are so convinced that the devil is a liar regarding their destiny. What a dynamic! Satan can try to mess the route but never be ultimate in matters of destiny. Regarding their victory they know he is a liar; regarding their future they stick to the promises of God and stick long enough to see their victories take effect. It is Jesus' will that man never give up but always pray, **Luke 18:1.**

Jesus taught us a very valuable lesson marking an essential element to the dynamics of apostolic people: A woman in the text persisted until an unjust ruler acted on her behalf to her good. It took persistence not the larky approach of the immature to be always on the lose, lose end of engagements – apostolic people fight. The devil likes to distort the truth by always telling us that our prayers are not being heard. It has been his trick perpetually to discourage the saints from the time of creation, and he won't stop until we stop him.

To Eve he said, "Did God really say"; to Daniel he kidnapped the angel who had been sent with the answer to his prayers. His trick is to destroy, delay and distort and he doesn't change his colors. As an apostolic person open your eyes and see the patterns and trends in your life and act decisively. Put Satan in his place he is a loser. Delay after all is never denial, we will break loose in Jesus' name. He can come and lie to you that your deliverance or healing is a miss; his intentions are to sow doubt to your faith. Watch out for him. Resist him and he will flee from you, **James 4:7**. We have the word as our anchor to conquer Satan. Like Jesus we use and quote the word and it works so well. Satan knows scripture and he won't want to mess around verses and chapters of the Holy Book!

We must always counter him with scriptures. His lies must not be left unchallenged; if a lie goes unchallenged it ceases to be a lie[27]. Let the kingdom people learn to say, "No " to the devil's tricks and gain victory each moment a temptation or attack comes – this is our victory. Always be alert, on the offensive putting on the belt of truth and the breastplate of righteousness. The whole armory of **Ephesians Chapter 6** is a daily dress. I and my children at COAN Gilead we agreed that from 2018 going forward we gonna be a threat to the devil, fulfilling our apostolic dynamic as soldiers of Christ.

Apostolic people know their position in Christ and their position in the family (Kingdom of God). They live out their faith as sons in the kingdom, not as hired servants or guests, but sons with a spirit of ownership. They appreciate the principles governing son-ship, this is a dynamic often abused by sons in the ministry. The early church could have died if the apostles ha d no sons in the ministry who took the bullet for their fathers vice versa the fathers for the sons. I devoted a long time to this in my MBS project, where I spoke about the topic of Modern Day Ecclesia Deception. The same subject is also coming in my next book on Revival in our day. We need true sons in the ministry.

True sons receive ministry in abundance from their fathers and with open hearts they learn from them. They are natured as a holy seed, just as a good farmer natures his crops with a definite expectation of growth. The word will never be void in its agenda if received with willing hearts. Jesus' Parable of the Sower is a good starting point to understand this dynamic. Isaiah brings the depth that the word once received, will not go back void without meetings its purpose in a willing heart and a yielding soul, **Isa 55:10.** So is my word; God is saying success is in His word, obeyed and followed.

Apostolic people are anointed, they carry power from above, the Acts Report is a perfect example. Jesus said, I have given you authority, to trample down snakes and scorpions and overcome all the power of the enemy, and nothing will harm you, **Luke 10:19.** This is a very crucial text to embolden us in the reality of the Christian pilgrimage. With Christ dwelling richly in our hearts make apostolic people a real threat to the enemy's kingdom. We have always been a threat to each other because of our salvation, but we must now study and grow in spiritual muscles in order to garner those kingdom victories. The word is the source of all spiritual victories, devotion to scripture is a sure sign of a mature apostolic believer.

---

[27] Abraham Lincoln in Lincoln on Leadership, Donald T Phillips

Another dynamic of the apostolic people is prayer; the love for prayer. Prayer is always a sign that one believes in God, if you don't pray, you don't believe - if you don't believe you also don't pray. I normally say, opening your mouth is a good starting point to consistent engagement with the divine. Apostolic people make decrees with their mouths; they speak what they believe. They know that death and life is in the power of the tongue. Solomon says, ''they that love the tongue (*speaking/talking*) shall eat the fruit thereof, our emphasis. We have shared about prayer in depth in another chapter in this book,

Apostolic People: The Dynamics

➢Anchored on the Early Church Model: **Acts 2:1.**
➢Exhibit the Acts of The Apostles,
➢Having Dynamic Faith in God,
➢And a Dynamic Conviction in the Word.
➢Demonstrate Dynamic Commitment to The Call.
➢Dynamic Demonstration of Power – **Acts 3;4;**
➢An Apostolic Drive, are passionate for God
➢Devoted to the Apostles Teachings;
➢Give themselves first to God, **2 Cor 8;**
➢Then to their apostles in accordance with God's will:

TOGETHER is the watchword for a Spirit led church –they walk the faith together as a Holy Spirit led family, nation or marriage - TOGETHER. A lot can happen for the apostolic seed when they are together, united and walking in the same spirit. At the Upperroom, Holy Spirit descended in dramatic fashion when they were with one accord, in **John 17** Jesus told his people to be together (one, united) so that the world will know they are His disciples. The Trinity is the best example of unity we can evener find, God the Father, God the Son and God the Spirit are one. Whatever they plan comes to pass. Do we want success for the church, do we need miracles in our midst, let us be untied and worship in one accord and see Jehovah daring all.

The devil is too quick to celebrate your failure; give him no room. Apostolic people have moved from average Christian living to the supernatural and extraordinary. The devil now knows them, try he may but he is aware that inside is an abundance of the word and that he will not win the fight. Our victory was settled at Calvary. No matter how many battles, the chorus is always victory, for in Christ every promise of God is a 'Yes and Amen' to the glory of God. Apostolic people are enlightened regarding their inheritance in God, they have taken over and proudly declare; Never Again, even in the face of seemingly impossible situations:

MY NEVER AGAIN' APOSTOLIC CONFESSION

Never Again Will I Say 'I Can't' Because I Can Do All Things Through Christ Jesus: Philippians 4:13.

Never Again Will I Say "I Don't Have" Because My God Shall Supply All My Needs According to His Riches
Philippians 4:19.

Never Again Will I Say "I Am Afraid" Because God Has Not Given Me a Spirit Of Cowardice But a Spirit of Power
2 Timothy 1:7.

Never Again Will I Say "I Lack Faith" Because God Has Given to Every Man A Measure of Faith: Romans 12:3*

Never Again Will I Say "I Am Weak" Because The Lord is The Strength of My Life: Psalm 27:1.

Never Again Will I Say "Satan Is Powerful" Because Greater is The God That Is in Me Than The Evil in The World
1 John 4:4.

Never Again Will I Say "I Am Defeated" Because I am More Than a Conqueror Through Christ Jesus: Romans 8:37.

Never Again Will I Say "I Lack Wisdom" Because Christ Has Become For Us The Wisdom of God: 1corinthians 1:30.

Never Again Will I Say "I Am Sick" Because Through His Stripes We Are Healed: Isaiah 53:5.

Never Again Will I Say "I Am Burdened" Because I Cast All My Burdens Upon Jesus Who Cares for Me: 1 Peter 5:7.

Never Again Will I Say "I Am in Bondage" Because Where The Spirit of The Lord is There is Freedom
2 Corinthians 3:17.
Never Again Will I Say "I Am Condemned" Because There is No Condemnation For Those Who Are In Christ Jesus: Romans 8:1.

CHAPTER 10
DYNAMICS OF AN APOSTOLIC PEOPLE 2
'A People Of Prayer'

I do teach frequently on the subject of prayer but will never claim to exhaust the subject. It is fair to say that each Bible teacher will have their go and leave the rest to others. I am going to inspire and motivate you to pray in this section. As apostolic people we are in deed and lifestyle a people of prayer. To open it up: "Just open up your mouth and pray, it will be just fine and you will be heard''. And spare me the theology, spare me the religion, and spare me the knowledge of this world and just allow me to open my mouth to pray; this is a statement of focus and intend from the seeker after God. Doors shall be opened, the opportunities will come and those tears shall not be in vain.

No man can shut a door that God wants to open, and no person can open a door that God wants to shut. It is through conversation with Him that we shall be able to know His will for our lives and access his master-plan for our personal well being. We will explore ahead and analyze some seven powerful prayers from the Bible. If you ever feel at a loss for what to pray, there's no better guidebook for petitions to our Heavenly Father than the very book He wrote - the Bible. Almost every book in there contains a plea or request, and page after page points to another reason why we need to pray and call upon a God whose capabilities are endless. It is a joy to turn our weaknesses to a God who has none.

So, when you feel like you just don't have strength, inspiration or even words, turn first to the Word. Although we could list hundreds of prayers, we plucked out seven of our favorites to show just how filled to the brim the Bible is with ways to call upon our great God. It is legal to pray; it is godly to call upon the divine in all circumstances; it is God's will that His people converse with Him as children, as servants and as subjects desiring mercy. Welcome to the world of apostolic and prophetic prayer. The Lord has granted us permission and there is before us an open door to pray and all kinds of prayers will make a difference. Scripture teaches us to pray all kinds of prayers:

(i)   Prayer for Healing; it is our portion in God.
(ii)   Prayer for Strength; when you feel weak, God is always strong.
(iii)   Prayer for Protection: Trusting Jehovah Shammah.
(iv)   Scheduled Prayers: Morning, Afternoon and Evening; the Hebrew schedule is still very good.
(v)   Good Night Prayers; putting your soul in God's hand.

(vi)   The Prayer of Jabez; a model prayer for deliverance.
(vii)   The Lord's Prayer; the most powerful prayer in the universe.
(viii)   The Prayer of ………………….. Put your Name there.
(ix)   Serenity Prayer; when in confusion, or not understanding something.
(x)   Event prayers; praying for a specific event.
(xi)   The Sinner's Prayer; the first prayer ever.
(xii)   Prayer for Forgiveness; seeking holiness.
(xiii)   Prayer for Guidance: a sign of Trust in God' direction.
(xiv)   Intercessory Prayer - praying for others.
(xv)   Apostolic Prayers and Blessings.
(xvi)   Aggressive Prayers - Violent Prayers.
(xvii)   Christmas Prayers – For Christ's sake.
(xviii) Thanksgiving Prayer; Praising God for His works.
(xix)   Spiritual Warfare – embracing the amour of God.
(xx)   Easter Celebratory Prayers- Christ Matters.
(xxi)   Mother/father's Day Prayer –Honoring parents.
(xxii)   Prayers for My Husband - my Wife –Marriage.
(xxiii) Prayers for My Children – for Family.
(xxiv)   Prayer of Prayers – A revisit and realignment, repetition or copying model prayers.

These are veritable prayers that mark an apostolic person and our praying should be anchored upon scriptural teaching and not vain babbling. It is not correct to live on chants and cultic myopic repetitions and assume we are praying. We do well take heed and speak the scriptures in our prayers. Knowledge is power, and scripture exhorts the saints to walk in knowledge for without it, people perish. So, always pray with knowledge. In that same vein of knowledgeable prayers, we will now attend to the seven powerful prayers in the Bible, analyzing them one by one to build you up in this most holy faith. Embrace them for a prayer revival upon your soul.

1. *The Lord's Prayer (Matthew 6:9–13)*

This prayer is the true classic that even non Christian religions know it by memory. Most of us have said this prayer and could likely recite it right now. But there is much more to this model that Jesus gave us than just rote recitation. It is a life transforming and heaven shaking prayer. This is a prayer with real power: it speaks of God's kingdom coming, God's will being done on earth, and all that we need for each day. It's truly power packed; where else could we go as apostolic people for a model prayer for all circumstances. So, let us all in devotion and adoration take a closer look at what it teaches: there is no better prayer, no powerful petition nor any praying that beats this one.

"Our Father in heaven,
hallowed be your name.
Your Kingdom come,
your will be done,
on earth as it is in heaven.
Give us this day our daily bread,
and forgive us our debts,
as we also have forgiven our debtors.
And lead us not into temptation,
but deliver us from evil." (Matthew 6:9–13)

What genius of Biblical asset; here is the simple prayer of our Lord that touches everything about us, about God and His Kingdom and about all that prayer should contain. There is in it praise; there is acknowledgement of God's greatness; an appreciation of the Kingdom and an expression of man's daily needs. There in it also lie the conviction that God's will is ultimate and it has to be hastened with holy awe; that as heaven is littered with the knowledge of God so should it be on earth.

As God rules the heavens and the earth, so the earth must reflect the hand of the divine. Jesus instruct us to ask for forgiveness, and to forgive others in one sentence, to ask for the cancellation of the spiritual debt, and that God's hand may guide us not into temptation but deliver us from the evil which abounds in the earth wherein we sojourn. Now the adoration: the power and the glory, forever and ever. Amen. Let each one of us learn this prayer by heart and teach it to our children from tender ages, so that when they grow up they will not depart from it. Ascribe Glory to His name Oh Ye peoples. Nothing beats this prayer in terms of power, O glorious Christ.

2. Jonah's Prayer for Salvation (Jonah 2:2–9)

Our second port is the evangelistic book of Jonah, I call it so. We may never be swallowed by a great fish, but we can still experience the shame and regret that Jonah felt after he tried to run away from God's assignment. The prophet's plea to the Father provides a poignant scaffolding for our own prayers of repentance. And remember that God heard and answered this humble, honest prayer: you too in penitence shall be heard and answered, no matter how off road you may have gone, even already in Tarshish, God will consider your return with open arms.

There goes Evangelist Jonah:

"In my distress I called to the Lord,   and he answered me.
From deep in the realm of the dead I called for help,
and you listened to my cry.
You hurled me into the depths,   into the very heart of the seas,   and the currents
swirled about me;
all your waves and breakers swept over me.
I said, 'I have been banished from your sight;
yet I will look again toward your holy temple.'

The engulfing waters threatened me,   the deep surrounded me; seaweed was wrapped
around my head.
To the roots of the mountains I sank down;
the earth beneath barred me in forever.
But you, Lord my God, brought my life up from the pit.
"When my life was ebbing away, I remembered you, Lord,
and my prayer rose to you, to your holy temple.

"Those who cling to worthless idols   turn away from God's love for them. But I, with
shouts of grateful praise,
will sacrifice to you. What I have vowed I will make good.
I will say, 'Salvation comes from the Lord.'"

What a prayer; what a repentant heart Jonah proved before Jehovah. The man had boarded a ship aloof to Tarshish, assuming God would not catch up with him. However the will of the Lord prevails, no-matter how we may try to circumvent his purposes. A big fish swallowed up Jonah after the seafarers had had enough of him and he confessed being the reason why the ship was in trouble. He requested to be thrown into the sea to die for all instead. This was a good sign that evangelist Jonah still had others at heart, though he didn't fancy any success preaching to the in Ninevittes.

The Jonah prayer came when he realized that he could not run away from God and that he was not going to die until he do the will of God. We as apostolic people know that God will accept us if we return. We turn back in holy surrender He still keeps His arms opened wide to a rebellious brood, how lucky, how graced, how favored we are. This agrees with the invitation in Isaiah, "Even if your sins are as red as scarlet, come unto me and I will wash you as white as snow" Reading this passage you may be backslidden and far from the Lord or planning to exit the faith due to one of many reasons, 'He says return' and will you?

3. David's Prayer for Deliverance (Psalm 3)

This one was a tough choice because the Psalms are stuffed full of cries groaning, celebratory prayers and various petitions. If you ever want a primer for prayer, you can't go wrong with this wisdom book. But we chose **Psalm 3** because it provides a concise portrait of crying out to God in the midst of great stress. David's words are no less relevant to our modern workplace and lifestyle as they were to his battles: it is our sure heritage to embrace the ancients' souls as models to our spiritual edification.

''Lord, how many are my foes! How many rise up against me!
Many are saying of me, "God will not deliver him."
But you, Lord, are a shield around me,   my glory, the One who lifts my head high.

I call out to the Lord,   and he answers me from his holy mountain.
I lie down and sleep;   I wake again, because the Lord sustains me.
I will not fear though tens of thousands   assail me on every side. Arise, Lord!
Deliver me, my God! Strike all my enemies on the jaw;
break the teeth of the wicked.
From the Lord comes deliverance.
May your blessing be on your people''

We all have enemies and haters; jealousy and envy rearing ugly heads at whatever may be of us. David faced similar. How the Psalmist shifts from crying in weakness to declaring what His God is able to achieve we can only wonder. Indeed He is a wonder working God: He calls the weak to declare themselves strong because of his name and his covenant with them. He says He is our refuge and our strength, even in distress like David was. David confidently instructs God to strike His enemies: would you take a moment to instruct your able God to strike all your enemies right now in the name of Jesus. We are reminded of his son's declaration in **Proverbs 18:10,** ''The name of the Lord is a strong tower; the righteous run to it and they are safe'. Yes, and the musician echoes; 'blessed be the name of the Lord'

4. Hannah's Prayer of Praise
(1 Samuel 2:1–10)

It is not often that testimonies just come before trials; we have to face the tests of life and pass them then we can have testimonies and the singing of joy. When Hannah received the child she begged God for, her first instinct is to praise the One who provided. She wants to thank Him for His greatness and His deliverance.

Too often we pray before receiving, but then forget to pray after God answers. Let this prayer guide you in thanksgiving and appreciation :

"My heart exults in the Lord; my horn is exalted in the Lord.
My mouth derides my enemies, because I rejoice in your salvation.
"There is none holy like the Lord: for there is none besides you;
there is no rock like our God. Talk no more so very proudly,
let not arrogance come from your mouth; for the Lord is a God of knowledge, and by him actions are weighed.

The bows of the mighty are broken, but the feeble bind on strength.
Those who were full have hired themselves out for bread,
but those who were hungry have ceased to hunger.

The barren has borne seven, but she who has many children is forlorn. The Lord kills and brings to life; he brings down to Sheol and raises up. The Lord makes poor and makes rich;
he brings low and he exalts. He raises up the poor from the dust; he lifts the needy from the ash heap to make them sit with princes and inherit a seat of honor. For the pillars of the earth are the Lord's, and on them he has set the world''

"He will guard the feet of his faithful ones, but the wicked shall be cut off in darkness, for not by might shall a man prevail. The adversaries of the Lord shall be broken to pieces;
against them he will thunder in heaven. The Lord will judge the ends of the earth; he will give strength to his king and exalt the horn of his anointed."

Thus Hannah became one of the great among the ancients, not only in her praying but in the manner of God's answer. She also created a rich testimony by handing over the son born to her first as a priest unto the Lord in fulfillment of her promise to God. He had given, He deserved Samuel more than Hannah. And God continued to open her womb and more kids came from the barren woman. Oh that God would raise for us Hannahs in each generation, that we may see such marvelous deeds of the divine meeting faithful souls.

5. Hezekiah's Prayer
2 Kings 19:14-19 New International Version (NIV[28])

---

[28] Public Domain, online Editions

[14]" Hezekiah received the letter from the messengers and read it. Then he went up to the temple of the Lord and spread it out before the Lord.[15] And Hezekiah prayed to the Lord: "Lord, the God of Israel, enthroned between the cherubim, you alone are God over all the kingdoms of the earth. You have made heaven and earth. [16] Give ear, Lord, and hear; open your eyes, Lord, and see; listen to the words Sennacherib has sent to ridicule the living God.

[17] "It is true, Lord, that the Assyrian kings have laid waste these nations and their lands. [18] They have thrown their gods into the fire and destroyed them, for they were not gods but only wood and stone, fashioned by human hands. [19] Now, Lord our God, deliver us from his hand, so that all the kingdoms of the earth may know that you alone, Lord, are God."

Much has been said about Hezekiah and we will interest ourselves with him briefly here: Hezekiah and Israel had messed up the covenant but God forgave them. God who is rich in mercy will not abandon forever. Hezekiah in greater part had done good and walked in the ways of his fathers, and God could not forget that such that He sent Isaiah with a judgment reversal message.

Hezekiah's prayer and humility before defeated death. Your prayers as an apostolic person can defeat death or delay the day of your death. Neither you; your children nor your kinsmen are doomed for destruction; God has a better deal for the elect of whom you are. Walk in the fear of God, be circumspect, remember the good ways of the Lord, and when challenging times come, pray meaningful prayers and reap the dividends.

6. Battleground Prayer.
Psalms 35:1-7
''Plead my cause, O Lord, with them that strive with me: fight against them that fight against me.

[2] Take hold of shield and buckler, and stand up for mine help.

[3] Draw out also the spear, and stop the way against them that persecute me: say unto my soul, I am thy salvation.

[4] Let them be confounded and put to shame that seek after my soul: let them be turned back and brought to confusion that devise my hurt.

Let them be as chaff before the wind: and let the angel of the Lord chase them.

[6] Let their way be dark and slippery: and let the angel of the Lord, persecute them.

[7] For without cause have they hid for me their net in a pit, which without cause they have digged for my soul.

[8] Let destruction come upon him at unawares; and let his net that he hath hid catch himself: into that very destruction let him fall''

And Moses alluded, ''Suffer not a witch to live'' we get that in **Exodus 22:18'**, an implication that witches were supposed to be killed in Israel. David echoed revenge; let them be ensnared by their own net – more like let them drink their own poison. Those who hid a net for me may they themselves be entangled, let them fall into the pit they have dug for me. This is combat praying: the witch must die. Even in our day, our words have power to deal with all evil. We can instruct God to deal with our enemies, or simply release the angelic host to fight the battles for us. We have the name and the blood of Jesus, the word, our faith, and ever present Holy Spirit as weapons of our warfare.

Death and life is in the power of the tongue and they that love it shall eat the fruit thereof. Your words are arrows, they are bullets. Speak forth war and destruction upon your enemies, not only after they have set a net for you, Nay; a snake is killed not because of what it has done; it must die because it's a snake. The same with demons; as apostolic people we all know demons have no mercy; they can kill at any given moment. A critical look at the mess Satan is causing upon mankind is a sure reminder that once found the snake must die. We are ordained to crush the head of the serpent, we follow in Jesus' footsteps in fighting the battles of the Kingdom. Our secret arsenal is knowledgeable prayer

7. The Prayer of Jabez (1 Chronicles 4:10)
When the author of Chronicles dutifully provides us with a list of Judah's descendants, he can't help but stop himself. Right in the midst of all these names, he comes to Jabez, a man he wants us to notice, a man of true honor. How honorable Jabez was the Bible does not tell; we only hear of the agony he caused his mother at birth and that he was a man of sorrows and trouble because of his name. But God, who is always rich in mercy, turns the tables when a willing heart presents petitions. If you've ever felt like you've caused pain or if you've ever wanted to believe that God can do more than you can ask or imagine, this prayer is for you:

"Jabez cried out to the God of Israel, 'Oh that you would bless me and enlarge my territory! Let your hand be with me, and keep me from harm so that I will be free from pain.' And God granted his request."
Simple? I do not think so; there were years of pain and affliction, there was his mother always reminding him of the pain he had caused at birth. His name was a memorial of his attachment to trouble. Jabez could not have been honorable, but underprivileged. Great testimonies come out of great trials. The power of God is made perfect in our

weaknesses, for when we are weak – we are strong. Pray the prayer of Jabez regarding that desire, that failing marriage, that folding business, for any death bed situation, the prayer of Jabez is a key. Just ask God to remember you and he will.

In closing this section I want to remind us to always bank on the fact that God has given us the green light to ask for anything we want; **John 14:27**, "Ask anything of the Father in my name and I will do it" And nothing in this world is immune to prayer! Prayer is a key and a key blocker: our words shape the world. (PUSH) Pray Until Something Happens, this statement has sustained many a believer in trying situations. When we pray, we touch the heart of God: we enter the supernatural void and converse with the divine. Never underestimate the power of prayer.

Apostle James says, ''is any among you afflicted? Let him pray. Is any merry, let him sing psalms. Is any sick among you? Let him call for the elders of the church; and let them pray over him, anointing him with oil in the name of the Lord: And the prayer of faith shall save the sick, and the Lord shall raise him up; and if he has committed sins, they shall be forgiven him. Confess your faults one to another, and pray one for another, that ye may be healed. The effectual fervent prayer of a righteous man availeth much. Elias was a man subject to like passions as we are, and he prayed earnestly that it might not rain: and it rained not on the earth by the space of three years and six months. And he prayed again, and the heaven gave rain, and the earth brought forth her fruit'' **James 5:13-18**. These are prayers for all occasions; for healing, for joy and celebration, for forgiveness and our blessing of and submission to spiritual authority. James ends with the fact that Elijah was a man like unto us, yet he prayed and nature obeyed him. We also can pray and nature will submit to our directive. We can reflect on may who prayed in the Bible and God came through for them, in fact the Bible does not report a prayer that was not answered. What an inspiration to us to open our mouths and Pray!

Just like Jabez was in trouble; yet he did the right thing that changed his destiny through prayer, you also can change your destiny through prayer. Hannah changed her testimony and territory, the barren woman sang after prayers were answered, your barrenness can also depart from your life in the name of Jesus. Jacob met god in prayer and even his name was changed, Jabez got a new name. Isaiah tells us of Beulah and Hephizbah, a seeming reference to the previously barren Hannah: these are darling names the Lord allots to those who come to him for transformation. Jacob had to pray all night and his prayer was intense such that an angel had to come and sustain him the whole night; his name change came after a soulful night of prayer. Prayer is effective and practical. And the Lord Jesus taught us to pray and not faint so we have to pray. Pray therefore without ceasing, in the Spirit and in all kinds of prayers.

CHAPTER 11

'KINGS AND PRIESTS'

"And hast made us unto our God kings and priests: and we shall reign on the earth".
REV 5:10 KJV.
It is God's desire that His people who walk in the apostolic order would rule on His behalf in the earth. The word says, "You are gods" referring to the children of God according to Psalms 82:6. There is a small 'g' to address the issue of blasphemy and harness our limitation but God wouldn't makes us into his image with less virtue than Himself, He contracted Himself to His word so we are full of God. Any variations would contradict His nature and faithfulness, so we are gods with sufficient capacity as God would like us to have in the assignment.

Every soul that accepts Christ is saved to royalty. Discipleship and training in Kingdom matters will help each one reach their full potential to reign in the earth as scripture commends us. Our King is Jesus: the King of Kings and Lord of lords. Yes, He hath made us sit with Him as vassals of the Great King, right there in heavenly places. We are royalty in God's sight; Peter says, "a royal priesthood, a holy nation and holy people called out of darkness into God's marvelous light" **1 Peter 3:9**. And He hath made unto us Kings and Priests unto our God and we shall reign in the earth, **Rev 5:10**, KJV. Note the narrative, Kings first; the Law of First Mention, and then Priests. So we are kings first and then priests in our service to God's Kingdom.

Kings: traditionally, royalty has been defined by the bloodline. Princes are born into it; it's a default position. It is more of a heritage than anything else. I have heard some royals in African languages acclaiming that they have no apology to make about being royals when criticism mounts on their well- publicized extravagancies; it is indeed true, there is nothing to apologize for. The elements ahead will create serious relational problem with those who may unfortunately find themselves on the opposite side of the royal bridge. We will also not apologize for being royals in God's Kingdom.

When I taught this message at the COAN Gilead's Royal Faith Tabernacle in Johannesburg I had six different nationalities in the service who helped with these African statements by royals:

Ndozvatiri – Shona;
Lena singobani – Zulu;
Dit is Wie Ons is – Afrikaans;

Izi Ndife Amene – Bemba;
Ndoomalevels acho – Shona slang
This is who we are – English.

And what are the marks of royalty? What are the pointers, what are the different characteristics that separate earthly royals from common people, there is an almost but different separation between spiritual royals and commoners. Knowing earthly definitions will help us appreciate spiritual packages. We can safely point to a few marks or attributes of royalty here:

A. Lifestyle: royals play with the stars, they live in quality, it's unbefitting for royals live lowly.
B. Wisdom – Royals walk circumspectly, redeeming the time, it is their precious asset. **Ps 78:72.**
C. Dress: Royals dress to kill, walking in bliss and bling in today's language.
D. Fighting spirit: attitude, royals get the best no-matter what, it's common among royals not to rest until an assignment is complete.
E. Special foods and delicacies, **Dan 1** – Royal Food is a mark; we also see the Queen of Sheba in awe when she saw the sitting and delicacies at Solomon's dinner table.
F. Honor and Esteem are ascribed wherever you go because of the name you carry: **Exodus 33: 18, Col 1:27.**
G. Royals are easily identifiable, they are popular and eminent. We cannot as apostolic people go into hiding: Jesus said,

We cannot hide our identity, we are set in grace as royals in God's house: ''A city built atop a hill cannot be hidden'' We are the salt and the light of the world. Spiritual royals bring meaning and purpose to mother earth, without us and our God the earth is void and doomed. Men do not light a candle to put it under a table, but on top so that it may give light, the same with us; we are God's ambassadors, we need to arise and take our stand. We have a call to let the world see God through us. So, no more hiding, shine forth as starts, be visible, walk with your head high as sons of the great King; the world awaits with groaning.

Developing upon this, and bring a clearer meaning and exposure of the above text allow us to share with you in the next section some seven elements of royalty that we believe will help us understand this position granted to us of the divine. It's no small matter, that we are priests and Kings unto our God. These elements link perfectly with the attributes we have just shared in the previous section as pointers to royalty. The list may not be exhaustive but, will help us for the purpose of this project; we can allow further study and development that will enrich this list:

The Seven Elements of Royalty

1. Royalty is Associated with **Authority and P**ower.
2. It's Associated with **Wealth**: Solomon says, 'The Rich will rule over the poor;
3. Associated with **Beauty**: Elegant regalias, bliss & show offs are custom to royals.
4. With **Glory**: An irresistible presence – we can't ignore the prince. Off cause divine glory overrides everything.
5. Marked by **Loyalty**: Patriotism and deep commitment are hallmarks of enduring dynasties.
6. Sustained by **Wisdom**: Diligence; a wise king is preferable in any kingdom, without it dominions can be lost, the throne can be stolen or hijacked.
7. Love – No domain will exist nor last without royal love to its people; even God is loved and adored as the Great King on account of His undying sacrificial love.

Are there any qualifications for royal status? Yes. But, it does not depend on the Prince or Princess, it is on the traditional bloodline and it was cast in place by the ancestors who fought battles and conquered to take domains. It is a privilege to be born into royal blood. Culture and tradition preserve royal status; ours is preserved by the blood of Jesus. Adam threw it away; but Jesus came and restored it through Christmas as we shared with you on the Christmas chapter. In salvation God started a new dynasty of royals as Christ's brothers came into the scene through the 'New Birth'.

John 1:12 says, "To all who received Him, He gave them the power to become children of God" That is a mystery, yet a reality of the elect. Our election is predetermined, but our entry into the household of the apostolic life must receive Jesus Christ as our personal Savior by faith. Our salvation is not about heaven only, it carries lots of benefits; primarily the right to become children of God. We receive a right through Christ to participate in matters of God's Kingdom. We are also in the traditional bloodline of God's elect through the in-washing of the blood of Jesus. The blood of the lamb purchased us (redeemed) back to God. Our salvation is like a being born into it; the covenant was there before us.

He hath made us Kings and priests unto our God, and we shall reign in the earth. We concurred that Kingship is mentioned first, looking with the lens of the Law of First Mention we can assume that Kingship is primary in running the earth. As kings we are rulers, we are authority, judges, and lawmakers of the domain. We make the decrees that change courses and cause things to be as we open our mouths governing, not only the earth but the whole universe. Even things that are not, become, as we speak in faith and divine inspiration. Our God uses words to create, therefore as His offspring we also believe and we speak.

As Priests we are ministers of the covenant and sustainers of the kingdom. We are the salt and the light of the earth; as we live out our inherent faith we give direction to the world. The world cannot move forward without priests. The King and the priest need each other. And the two have distinguished roles in scripture; we see Saul, David, Jehu, Solomon, Nebuchadnezzar, Cyrus etc having varied specific divine assignments. They are divine appointees in as much as we also are. These kings can provide a perfect picture of God's rule.

We as apostolic people have been given dual roles; and it is mainly by gifting; others will be Kings, others priests, yet others still both King and priest at the same time. I would like to believe I have been called to be a King and Priest at once. I only am discovering now through revelation, maturity and deeper study of the word of God. I have always assumed I was a priest only. The New Testament priest is ordained by God in salvation to administer the earth in matters pertaining to the spiritual kingdom slightly differing from the OT whereby he was to administer both the church and the government directly.

Original languages denote a priest as an administrator in God's house. That is why Jesus is called High Priest or the administrator of a new covenant. It refers to someone who officiates or performs certain specific duties.[29] In a way it's someone who causes certain things to come to pass; that's a prophet or apostle in essence. Moses led the 'Exodus', a term used for the exit of Israel out of Egypt. Samuel brought spiritual revolution to Israel. Ezra and Nehemiah partnered to rebuild the walls of Jerusalem, one acting as king and the other a priest. The army could not attempt to regroup in captivity and restore the kingdom, but these two did it. It was a specific role for the priests and not a political endeavor.

John the Baptist as a priest prepared the way for the coming of Christ yet his daily ministry was a constant confrontation with the King. It actually led him to execution as he delivered what politicians did not want to hear; the advent of a new kingdom. As apostolic people we are faced with a choice to either stand up for God's Kingdom or go with the world; John chose God. Politicians are also God's emissaries, but usually so carnal, off-road and in affront to God, and evil dominate their thrones. We stand in the gap for them; our reign is seasoned with righteousness and God will not

---

[29] Dickson Teachers' New Testament, 21st Century Revised King James Version. Rodger E Dickson, Africa International Missions 2006, Cape Town

abandon us when faced with any issues that pertain to His Kingdom. NT priesthood is based mainly spiritual gifting:

(i)   **1 Cor 12:7** – gifts given for the common good
(ii)   **Romans 12** – spiritual ennoblements
(iii)   **Ephesians 4:11** – the backbone of spiritual gifts commonly called the five-fold ministry because of the number five of gifts.

The secret of the gifting aspect is that when God meets committed man, anything is possible. He uses the despised things of this world to shame the wise. David acted as both King and priest, **2 Samuel 24:24**, yet upon selection he was least and last on Jesse's mind, but God had other ideas. The same David also acted out an eternal priestly role in writing the countless Psalms we have in the Bible after destroying the giant Goliath. What a heritage we have in the Psalms: what a compilation of both royal art and priestly adoration.

We are Kings so let us embrace Kingdom participation, our core being is God like; let us manifest in running the world. God wants us to be like him always. Let us walk as such, acting and living out our inherent nature as God's offspring. Let us believe in who we are and exhibit it - all creation awaits with eager anticipation for the royals to manifest. Walk in the glorious life to which you were called, make no apology in calling God your dad. Stick out and claim it on the hilltops and rooftops, Abba Father! We will close with the decrees that mold us into the image God desires. David yet again prophesies upon the Prince and we adopt the Psalm for it is for us a treasured spiritual heritage:

Psalms 72 'Royal Confessions'

1. I am Royalty, I am a child of the Most High;
2. I will judge with righteousness, I will serve the needy in my generation;
3. I will break to pieces the oppressor.
4. I shall be a terror to my enemies as long as the sun and moon endure.
5. My days will flourish and have abundance of peace.
6. I will have dominion from sea to sea.
7. May those who dwell in the wilderness bow before me; and my enemies shall lick dust.
8. May foreigners bring presents to me: strangers shall offer me choice gifts.
9. May I be a compassionate King in God's Kingdom;
10. May my life be far from violence.
11. May I live long, even longer than my enemies.

12. May I outlive the sun and the moon.
13, My the gold of Sheba come to me;
14. May prayers be made continually for me even by people I do not know.
15. May I find kingdom favor, even before God and before man.
16. May I be the man of the hour all my days and live in plenty, and not in want;
17. I will see the goodness of the Lord in the land of the living, **Ps 27:13**.
18. May my days be days of abundance, never any dull moment!
19. May I flourish like the forests of Lebanon, financially, in my career, profession, business, marriage, everywhere may I flourish all my days.
20. May my name be held in honor, as I walk in honor!
21. May uncommon doors open for me, may I receive the Prince's Worth in Jesus' Name!

As Apostolic People we Sing;

''Kings n' Priests We Are''
Saved to Royalty Our Call
Onward W' Jesus Christ We Reign;
Rein in the Earth O Ye Royals'
Reign, Reign, Oh Reign in e earth O Ye Royals'

He Being King of Kings, and He Lord of Lords,
Hath Made Us gods - As God Among Gods!

With This We Shout, "Dominion Is Ours'
An Echo to His Glorious Name'
So shall it be, So shall T Be
Amen and Amen.

He Being King of Kings, and He Lord of Lords,
Hath Made Us gods - As God Among Gods!

CHAPTER 12
THE GOD OF THE APOSTOLIC PEOPLE 1
"He Exceeds Expectations"

The Lord is my shepherd; I shall not want.
He maketh me to lie down in green pastures:
he leadeth me beside the still waters.
He restoreth my soul:
he leadeth me in the paths of righteousness for his name's sake.
Yea, though I walk through the valley of the shadow of death,
I will fear no evil: for thou art with me;
thy rod and thy staff they comfort me.
Thou preparest a table before me in the presence of mine enemies:
thou anointest my head with oil; my cup runneth over.
Surely goodness and mercy shall follow me all the days of my life:
and I will dwell in the house of the Lord forever.

Psalms 23, of David

The God of the apostolic people exceeds even His own people's wildest imaginations in doing good things. *"He Exceeds Expectations" and He Keeps On Doing Great Things" from generation to generation.* Much of the great things He does for His people are undeserved, what a God of mercy and compassion they serve! He keeps watch over His own and like a shepherd watches his sheep, so does he care for them. David gave us a complete picture when he wrote the above Psalm equating the Lord to a good shepherd in **Psalms 23.**

What a good God they serve! He keeps watch over His own with a hawk eye, lest some vulture might come and tear them in their vulnerability. He is our good shepherd: **Ps 23**; He knows my tomorrow and even all my needs before I come to him. It is becoming clearer now that there is no other god besides the God of the apostolic people. He is El Shaddai – the all sufficient God, a God with power and great love for His people. That brings us to the Hebrew words *'Parashat Lekha'* – meaning *nurturing love.* He is devoted to us because of His love nature; not because of anything we will ever do, no other God comes closer, if they be any gods.

In His might, nothing is difficult for Him; He has No impossibility. He says to Abraham, "Is anything too hard for the Lord? **Gen 18:14**. The same statement He repeated to Jeremiah, "Then came the word of the Lord unto Jeremiah, saying, Behold, am I not the Lord, the God of all flesh: is there anything too hard for me?" **Jeremiah 32:26 -28**[30]. He does the seemingly impossible to us. For with him nothing is indeed impossible: he has made the heavens and the earth with His outstretched arm and by His power. Our limitations should never stand in the way of God's unlimited capabilities.

He takes care of my enemies, in today's language we can safely say, "He has my back". He Exceeds Expectations. Let us for the next moments zero on the heart of Apostle Paul trying to explain God's capacity, "Now to Him who is able to do far more abundantly than all that we ask or think, according to the power at work within us, to him be glory in the church and in Christ Jesus throughout all generations, forever and ever. Amen" Let us establish the whole heart and context of not only the Great Apostle, but also of the inspirer, Holy Spirit, to be able to fully appreciate the depth of this characteristic of our God. We can do a mini analysis of the text verse by verse; the most common **verse 20** is a climax to a deeper discourse here.

Eph 3:14-20

On **verse 14** we hear Apostle Paul saying, "For this reason I bow my knees before the Father, continually. "For this reason" we have to deduce and identify the reason within the text. In early sections of **Chapter 3:1** Paul narrates the mystery. The text here now defines the mystery of our participation as the great mystery: Jesus is the mystery in whom all families in heaven and on earth derive their name. its right to believe that the apostolic people of whom this whole book is all about, the Kingdom Nation, The Body of Christ, or the Household of Faith – we derive our name from that mystery under the microscope; Jesus Christ, our Chief Apostle and High priest of the New Covenant. Here is Paul's defining of this Jesus;

(i)   from whom every family in heaven and on earth is named;
(ii)   that according to the riches of His glory He may grant you;
(iii)   to be strengthened with power through his Spirit in your inner being;
(iv)   so that Christ may dwell in your hearts through faith;
(v)   that you, being rooted and grounded in love, may have strength to comprehend;

---

[30] NIV is in public domain

(vi) with all the saints what is the breadth and length and
height and depth, and to know the love of Christ that surpasses knowledge, that you
may be filled with all the fullness of God. Jesus' love surpasses knowledge: so high
that you can't get over it, so wide you can't get around it, so
deep such that you can't get under it, it exceeds all expectations.

Apostle Paul clearly maintains that in Christ are glorious riches, and that we as God's
people are strengthened by them. Riches and glory speak of power and wealth. The
inner man is strengthened by the understanding and partaking of the mystery of Christ
which we have defined above. Paul prays for us that this mystery and revelation may
dwell richly in our hearts through our confession and acceptance of Christ. We are
expected to be established in love. The heart of the Apostle desires the Acts Model of
genuine love among brethren. That lays the perfect foundation for relationships: the
ability to discern and appreciate how wide, how long, how high and how deep is the
love of Christ. That love which surpasses knowledge and accomplishes the full
measure of God in us. Indeed that's why we say, "God is love".

The God of the apostolic people exceeds expectations. We see at the closure the
apostle Paul declaring, "Now unto him that is able to do exceeding abundantly above
all that we ask or think, according to the power that worketh in us. Unto Him be glory
in the church by Christ Jesus throughout all ages, world without end. Amen'' This is
God's grand design for us, that we walk in limitless power, unlimited knowledge and
all an encompassing love. This power is at work in us if we have:

- the right convictions
- the right confessions
- genuine salvation
- the right baptism
- the right Christ
- The right doctrine.

We need to have the right convictions about our God. Having wrong convictions
destroys the soul and religion becomes labor for nothing. Our confession must be
aligned aright; some see Christ as a small boy in Mary's hands, others prefer to use a
small letter when they refer to His Lordship; still others take his name in vain while
believing in other names. False religion and heresy will be with us as long as man
traverse the earth, but far be it from us as apostolic people to give in to heretic
doctrines; we have the word as our sure anchor. We will do well take heed unto it as
light that shines in a dark place and our God will shine on us.

We must have a genuine conversion experience; party to the Apostolic Creed is sure salvation based upon accepting the substitutionary death of Christ. It is by grace through faith, it is the salvation that Christ wrought on the cross, no other name can save. The attendant baptism must be scriptural aided by confession of faith in the word and His saving grace. With this truth in place, apostolic people have a license from Christ to do the works that he did on earth, even more according to **John 14:12**. Those are Jesus' own words, a snap in the face for ceasassionists who want to peddle the false doctrine that miracles ended with Jesus, hee, hee miracles ended with the early apostles is a statement of unbelief.

As Apostolic people, we know that we are represented by the Apostles and Prophets; that's our idea of Spiritual Son-ship. In as much as they are God's children, apostolic people understand the divine order spiritual fathers play a very important role in developing our talents, our gifts, and our very own destinies through mentorship, teaching and people development. There are protocols in the spiritual arena that cannot be circumvented for any reason whatsoever. In staying within divine order, the God of wonders exceeds all our expectations as he proves Himself faithful to the elect through miracles, signs and wonders.

True sons are submissive; they receive ministry in abundance **(Isa 55:10)** as a Holy Seed, watered by the word. They know in being in the right place in the Kingdom there is a benefit: power and might are granted without measure. They have Christ dwelling in their hearts as their sure anchor and source of hope with this they assume deep and not shallow spiritual endeavors. Their faith yearns to meet the Lord in all their adventures. It is the father's joy and responsibility to train the sons in righteousness, in the ways of the Lord and inspire great faith for achievements, the testimonies are coming keep the fire burning.

Let us go a bit deeper into the substance of this God of the apostolic people; God has so much power, so much influence, so much ability that it is impossible for Him to fail. He has transmitted the same power to his children, just like any loving father would share his skills and assets with his children. The Kingdom of God becomes the only kingdom to talk about.

'For the kingdom of God is not in word, but in power' **1 Cor 4:20**

2 Cor 10:3-5
''For though we walk in the flesh, we do not war after the flesh: the weapons of our warfare are not carnal, but mighty through God to the pulling down of strong holds; casting down imaginations and every high thing that exalteth itself against the

knowledge of God, and bringing into captivity every thought to the obedience of Christ'' KJV.

Our God exceeds expectations: He does not only offer salvation and access to heaven; he goes beyond and empower every saved soul spiritually. We are human beings yes, living and breathing like everyone else as regards this material world, but our composition is extra territorial. We now carry within us the spiritual element; we are alive to God. We are controlled by the Sprit of God hence our nature is supernatural. Apostle Paul says He has given us everything we need pertaining to life and godliness, everything we need. The spiritual is covered, the natural and material is covered. What a God we serve!

In spiritual battles we do not fight with the flesh and blood, nay, but our weapons are prayer, fasting, giving, sacrifices, love, and the leadership and guidance of Holy Spirit. The weapons we use are mighty through God. They are effective to the pulling down of strongholds, these are established demonic domains of opposition in spiritual realms. We also have the capacity through God to cast down all evil imaginations; and every high demonic force that may pretend to be something of a superpower in the heavenly places.

It is a truth that demons are pretenders, no imagination or opposing spirit stand a chance against the offspring and desire of God; all shall surrender and give glory for ultimate victory is for the children of God. For through us the whole earth shall be filled with the knowledge of God, as the waters cover the sea. No mercy upon the devil and let all believers stand up their ground, no mercy upon the devil and his cronies.

Let us quickly jump on to the next gem about our God of surprises and exceeding expectations. A God who is common is no God at all; ours breathes miracles, any movement of His is a miracles, He has the daily art of doing wonders. We are a people of His wonders in as much as we are the seed of the righteous.

'No Eye Have Seen, Nor Ear Heard'
1 Cor 2:9-10
''But as it is written, Eye hath not seen, nor Ear heard, neither have entered into the heart of man, the things which god hath prepared for them that love him. but god hath revealed them unto us by his spirit: for the spirit searcheth all things, yea, the deep things of God'' KJV[31]

---

[31] KJV Bible is in public domain

The God of the Apostolic people surprises me all the time; I am a recipient of his helping hand now and again even in instances I will not be expecting it, He chips in and rescues me. He exceeds expectations: He has given me air tickets right at the airport in response to faith; redemption in post life sickness and healed me when writing the Final Will seemed the last option.

Once I received my daughter from the dead, living the life of a volunteer, He has provided for me like a shepherd who knows his sheep are vulnerable and lost without him. What a caring God we serve: in His foreknowledge He surprises us. He is a God of new things, a God of new beginnings and a God of second chances. He is a God of restoration, a God who answers by fire and He exceeds even your wildest dreams.

What is your wildest imagination? What's your most extravagant dream or aspiration? What is your mountain like vision that people have said it cannot happen? Our God Exceeds expectations; keep believing it will happen. What is the grand threat facing your life right now? Speak back to it in faith and say, "My God can; who are you mountain? Before me ………………………………….. you shall be leveled! Confess it loudly, 'My God can do immeasurably, above all that I can ask, and all threats in my life are bluffing. Victory is mine. Hallelujah!

My God Can! My God Can! My God Can! That's my motto when the mountains mount and resistance increases, you can be of the same faith level and reap the rewards. For sure He can do all that a God with power can do. Who are you mountain? Before me _____ *(Write your name)* You shall be leveled. I am an apostolic seed and over you I shall prevail''

And regarding your enemy your God says in **Isa 54:17**, "no weapon that is fashioned against you shall succeed, and you shall refute every tongue that rises against you in judgment. This is the heritage of the servants of the Lord and their vindication from me, declares the Lord." What does it mean when it says, refuting tongues in judgment? Thou shall refute every tongue that rises against you in judgment''. To Refute in this context is to:
- Refuse.
- Renounce.
- Reject.
- Decline.
- Reverse.
- Block.
- Rebuff.

All these words related are action words, people of faith are active; faith has never been dormant nor docile. Faith leads us to rise up and challenge the status quo, to confront our enemy knowing full well the Lord is on our side. It is an affront to faith to be passive: our God did not give us a spirit of timidity, but of power, sound mind and sober judgment. We walk in confidence and speak back to the curse or resistance to our progress; we challenge the enemy at his game and are not afraid to get dirty for Kingdom manifests. Whoever digs a pit for me will fall into it and whoever sets a snare or hide a net for me will be entangled by their traps and I will have no apology to make about. 'No mercy', surfer not a witch to live!

And what about judgment in that text! A judgment in spiritual terms is a decree or, a declaration, it can be a curse, an effectual verbal bullet, or a pronouncement. When a curse or words of evil wish are spoken against us we do not just keep quiet and wait for the next curse, neither do we accept the judgment; no, we reverse it outright with our own words adopted from scripture. I like the Pentecostal warfare attitude and practice of send back to the sender, Yes, whoever sends a curse must feel the pain of their sorcery. It is important the for apostolic people to know every word in the Holy Book for it is our weapon for war.

Let us cap this discussion with power words, in judgment thou shalt refute:
- The devil says poor – you say Nope, I am rich;
- He says sick – You say I am Healthy, Wealthy and Happy:
- He says divorce – You say great and long lasting marriage:
- He says death – you say Grey hair shall be my portion:
- He says your loss: You shout my God of Restoration!
- He says restlessness – You say peace, **John 14:27.**
- Evil upon your children – you shall mine are not doomed for destruction but destined for the highest places.

God has given us the right to refuse anything Satan throws at us. Remember the **''NEVER AGAIN'' confessions!**

My Apostolic Declarations:

''I am heading for new things, I am facing new beginnings, I have been granted a second chance. I am moving into restoration. My God answers by fire, My God is exceeding all my dreams and my vision: my goals are coming up beyond my imagination in Jesus' name''

CHAPTER 13
THE GOD OF THE APOSTOLIC PEOPLE 2
'He Answers By Fire'

'A people of fire: We are many things to God, and He is many things to us: that's a mystery of the covenant. As fire, the Holy Spirit burns deep into our nature, purifying us of everything that contradicts the holiness of God. The fire of the Holy Spirit enables us to be the witness in our generation that He desires us to be. This fire only burns that which is contrary to the holy nature of God. We have dozens of incidents where fire stood for good, for His power, for his servants the saints, for the angels, for Holy Spirit, and for Christ. We are a Kingdom of fire.

We are a people of His fire; this is my inspiration in every moment of life. One preacher said that God is a livewire, so am I to the devil. We all as people of God must be ablaze with Holy Ghost fire. Timid and dry souls he desireth not. We must live the fire! A life with no sacrifice for God has no relationship with Him; souls must burn for God, not only do we need hot heads as we have in the churches, but also burning hearts that will change this world for God and for good. It takes fire in the soul: that fire of the Spirit which enables us to be witness in our generation. A living loving relationship with God will put us in the right position to be perfect representatives of the divine Kingdom, exhibiting holy awe and a Messianic passion; this is a pillar of apostolic living.

The man who comes to a right belief about God is relieved of ten thousand temporal problems, for he sees at once that these have to do with matters which at the most cannot concern him for very long; but even if the multiple burdens of time may be lifted from him, the one mighty single burden of eternity begins to press down upon him with a weight more crushing than all the woes of the world piled one upon another[32]. This is holy zeal; God begins to be all in all and His word the final authority over our life.

That mighty burden is his obligation to God. It includes an instant and lifelong duty to love God with every power of mind and soul, to obey Him perfectly, and to worship Him acceptably. This sums up holy Fire. And when this fire catches a willing soul, surely the world will note and change is inevitable for the power of God cannot fail nor falter. Jehu can be our prime example of a man ablaze with the fire of God. His

[32] AW Tozer, Paternoster Press, 1990. The Knowledge of the Most Holy

way became highways of destruction, construction and restoration. Men and women rallied behind this burning torch in God's hand and brought a significant revival upon Judah. Allow us to light your own internal fire at this turn with inspiring scriptures.

'Behold I do a new Thing …

If you always do what you have always done, you will always get what you have always got! Fire never leaves anything as it was before; there is either destruction, or enhancement, preservation or transformation – the same with the fire of God. If God is in it, the result will tell! There are a few pointers that I want us to note that are a result of the fire, or an essential component of the fire. When the fire is present, or desired we have a spiritual call to act in enabling ways to create the conducive environment for the manifestation of God's glory. We are active participants in the divine scheme: cold hearts are a playground for temptation and failure.

Weak Christians are not weak only in mind, but primarily in spirit. Where there is fire, temptation comes, yes, but not to destroy, but to tempt: where there is no fire, temptation comes to finish off the dead soul. Shake thyself of those cold spiritual temperatures and attempt zones anew. If you always do what you have always done, for sure you will get what you have always got; who is ready for a shift?

Think Anew, Act Anew …

Break the limitations by a new approach to sacred things. A week in the mountain in prayer will not go unnoticed of the divine, a small sacrifice will help you grow into a spiritual giant, kingdom participation will enable the fire in others to rub onto your cold stumps. Change your approach to the spiritual life. As a man thinks, so is he, **Proverbs 23:7**. Change your mindset and approach to the things of God; you can be better than this. Life a life, don't just pass up the days. You can be a world changer if the fire of God is alight in your soul.

Apostolic people are not weak, just humble; they are not dumb, they are circumspect – meaning they are always ahead. Be a threat to the devil, not gullible a catch on his menu. Remember he prowls around, like a lion seeking someone to eat and gullible Christian is on the menu[33]. Catch the fire of God and let the world see you go aglow for the Kingdom, the devil is first to take note. This is a higher life, a life for which Christ died.

Remember we are exploring the apostolic people of **Ephesians 2:20**, as we dare the world with our identity in Christ. We are God's people and we have no apology to

---

[33] The Message Bible, 1 Peter 5:8

make for boasting in him. Scripture encourages; 'Let him who boats boasts in this, that he knows the Lord'. So literally boasting is allowed in scripture with terms and conditions being: boasting in the Lord. We can reflect again on **Romans 8:19**, that all creation is waiting with eager anticipation for the manifestation of the sons of God. How do we manifest without boasting? How do we show off our identity to all creation without the fire burning in us? How do we exhibit the Kingdom if we do not show off the nature and characteristics of an apostolic people?

I reckon the hills and the mountains; the rivers and the seas, the animals that creep and those that fly all are groaning (KJV) for our manifestation. Probably because we were created last, I don't know! Yet still another dimension unfolds: all creatures are spiritually animate: the Psalms talk of the hills and mountains resonating with the voice of the divine; the rivers and the skies clapping, he speaks of the deep that roars; the trees that speak and the lands that cry. Why the animate connotation? Because God knows everything He created must have some way of feedback to the hand of the divine. The Lord Jesus supported my theory when He said, 'If we do not manifest in praise, God would ask the stones to get into praise'

Where is our scriptural backing for our God being a fire; of us being a people of His fire! Indeed God has revealed Himself more as fire than anything else in recorded history. Let us take a snap look at the evidence; **Deuteronomy 4:24**: 'For the Lord thy God is a Consuming Fire, even a jealous God'. Israel was being warned regarding trifling with the Hebrew God, who has also become our God. **Hebrews 12:29**: ''For our God is a consuming fire – thus echoes the writer of the Book of Hebrews.

Fire is one of our most important tools, and holds a prominent place in many ancient philosophies and religions. The ancient Greeks believed that fire – along with earth, water, and air was one of the four essential elements that made up the world. We now know that the world is a lot more complicated than that, with over a hundred elements of matter which can be combined in tremendous variety of ways. So, what exactly is fire?

In various senses, we speak of raging fire, of wild fire, fast fire, bonfire, infernos and blazes, flames, conflagration and combustion. All these are reference to fire in various forms. We can add in lighting, glory, sparks, etc. We can learn a lot from science in order to fully harness our spiritual kingdom. An understanding of each and every type of fire can be a beneficial way to develop the world and save humanity and nature. Out-of-control fires can cause unbelievable devastation.

But, we also cannot adequately tell the story of the Bible without talking about fire. The fire of the Bible speaks of various things among them:

- God's Wrath
- God's Glory
- God's Power
- God's Judgment
- God's love
- God's Spirit
- God's Presence
- God's Voice and many other attributes of the divine.

We cannot exhaust all of them as this volume is intended to reveal only that which supports our endeavor to define and exhibit the apostolic people; more so their God in this chapter. Everywhere you look, you see fire or the evidence of fire in the Bible. Let us begin with the first fire experience man had with God. **Exodus 3:2** we see Moses is herding his father in law's animals in the mountains having ran away from Egypt in escape from the folly of having tried to hasten his calling.

God had to send him for training under Jethro and build his leadership *(shepherding)* heart with the animals. God can use anything to train us for his work. The Hebrew people while languishing in Egypt were like animals, they required a caring and mature leader, not a forty year old hasty lad who would kill at the appearance of a street fight. Moses had some growing and some learning to do in order to fit the bill. He also needed a burning bush to deal with his faith. God trains us before sending us to any assignment.

Moses goes up the mountain as usual with his herd; faithful a shepherd he was such that his master had given him his own daughter in marriage. That was a sign Jethro never wanted to lose Moses. He sure must have matured by this time. Having spent those many years under Jethro, God wanted the real Moses to now rise up as an apostle and go straight to deliver Israel. Nothing could draw his attention quicker than a fire; it was unusual to find fires in those bushes during that time of the year.

God as a consuming fire did something Moses couldn't understand, burning a bush without it burning out. To Moses this was automatically a mystery, having lived among and being in the company of pagan Jethro could have aided his skepticism and possible superstition. The fire required a closer examination. As he drew closer to the bush to investigate, God called out to him, "Moses, Moses, remove your sandals for the place wherein you stand is holy''. God's presence makes any place holy. Moses complied; being a Hebrew he knew the voice of God was not to be trifled with. That sounds like a mature and ready guy. Whatever else happened with that fire is no longer of interest; God is interested in Moses, Israel, the future generations of His people.

The voice instructed Moses what he had to do and a debate ensued. The same hasty man who killed a man in a street fight, is now cautious and questions God to the last test. He gave God some very good excuses why he shouldn't be sent to undertake such a very important assignment. God bullshitted his excuses and instructed him to go. What's in your hand, God asked' It's a stuff my Lord. Throw it down: ouch, from the fire to a snake. Moses was up for some chastening. Now pick up that snake. The rest is history, Moses was convinced and off he went to deliver Israel out of Pharaoh's hands. We can safely say we are a people of His fire from the unfolding drama

In the wilderness God led his people by a pillar of fire by night and a cloud by day. What more can we say about the God of the apostolic people. The moon and the stars were not sufficient; He wanted to be present Himself with his people. He desired an eternal demonstration to the chosen nation and a heritage to the future generations.

The Lord Jesus Himself in **Luke 18:1** said that man ought always to pray and not give up, and he gave the parable of the persistent woman who got her wishes from that wicked King. Why pray? Prayer is a burning fire. When apostolic people pray; it's a fire! Jesus was supporting the message of **Lev 6:12** that the fire of the altar must never go out, it's the prayer ministry that lights up the church and the kingdom of God. Prayer holds a key place in apostolic living. As we pray, we lighten up fires everywhere: fires of seasoning and fires of destruction upon our enemies. And here we are as people of His fire declare henceforth: Fire upon our enemies! The later can be classified under the fire of judgment. We will explore these fires further.

'The fire of Judgment; Genesis 19:24 *"Then the Lord rained upon Sodom and on Gomorrah brimstone and fire from the Lord out of heaven."* This was real, though serving as types of the future judgment upon the wayward and errand nations.
  (i)   God will judge the world and every evil person in the world on the last day.
  (ii)   Just because judgment does not happen immediately doesn't mean that it won't.
  (iii) Galatians 6:7 says *"Be not deceived, God is not mocked..."*
WHY? He burns his mocker and destroys His enemies.

Let us now look at **'The fire of Demonstration' 1 Kings 8:38**: *"Then the fire of the Lord fell, and consumed the burnt sacrifice, and the wood, and the stones, and the dust, and licked up the water that was in the trench."*

(i)   This is one of the most spectacular of the Old Testament miracles. Elijah on one side; the 400 prophets of Baal on the other. Out-numbered 400 to 1. How do we interpret those odds?

(ii)   Satan's greatest boast is that he is in the majority. He loves to play the numbers game.

(iii)   God's people have always been in the minority.

(iv)   Guess what? You plus God always outnumbers the majority!

(v)   The priests of Baal found that out. Their ceremonies were fantastic; their worship was sincere; their intentions were honest. It is just that their God had no intention to respond.

(vi)   Do not challenge God. He will declare himself among the heathen in fire manifests and some may be consumed.

(vii)   The prophets of Baal are not just a memorial, but a reminder that the God of the apostolic people is a live-wire, He answers by fire and does not take it lightly when people serve idols.

The God of Elijah did not stop there, we see again in **2 Kings 1**; Ahab had died and Ahaziah was in charge. He got a disease from which he died but before his death he sent messengers to consult a foreign god. The messengers could not reach the witch's shrine as Elijah was sent by God to meet them with a stern rebuke. **verse 3''**But the angel of the Lord said to Elijah the Tishbite, Arise, go up to meet the messengers of the king of Samaria, and say unto them, 'Is it because there is not a God in Israel, that ye go to enquire of Beelzebub the god of Ekron? Now therefore thus saith the Lord, Thou shalt not come down from that bed on which thou art gone up, but shalt surely die. And Elijah departed. Elijah's words sound like a burning furnace on the evil king.

'And when the messengers turned back unto him, he said unto them, 'Why are ye now turned back?' And they said unto him, 'There came a man up to meet us, and said unto us, Go, turn again unto the king that sent you, and say unto him, 'Thus saith the Lord, Is it not because there is not a God in Israel, that thou sendest to enquire of Beelzebub the god of Ekron? Therefore thou shalt not come down from that bed on which thou art gone up, but shalt surely die. And he said unto them, 'What manner of man was he which came up to meet you, and told you these words? And they answered him, 'He was an hairy man, and girt with a girdle of leather about his loins. And he said, 'It is Elijah the Tishbite.

The king knew Elijah by personal description, by deed and by word: how he failed to hearken could only have been a divine strategy to do some demonstration of His fire. ''Then the king sent unto him a captain of fifty with his fifty. And he went up to him: and, behold, he sat on the top of an hill. And he spake unto him, Thou man of God, the king hath said, Come down'. And Elijah answered and said to the captain of fifty, 'If I be a man of God, then let fire come down from heaven, and consume thee and thy fifty'. And there came down fire from heaven, and consumed him and his fifty.

Again also he sent unto him another captain of fifty with his fifty. And he answered and said unto him, 'O' man of God, thus hath the king said, 'Come down quickly. And Elijah answered and said unto them, 'If I be a man of God, let fire come down from heaven, and consume thee and thy fifty'. And the fire of God came down from heaven, and consumed him and his fifty. All sane persons could agree this was the time the king either stopped the quest or went on his knees to entreat Elijah's God, but alas, he continued his defiance.

And he sent again a captain of the third fifty with his fifty. The evil King cares not of the perishing innocent warriors, he is not willing to acknowledge his evil intentions before God; why keep calling the prophet down yet he is showing God's wrath openly? This is not legend but an accurate scriptural narrative, written for out benefit, we better watch our steps lest in some manner we may invite the wrath and consuming fire of the Lord upon us and our armies.

And the third captain of fifty went up, and came and fell on his knees before Elijah, and besought him, and said unto him, 'O man of God, I pray thee, let my life, and the life of these fifty thy servants, be precious in thy sight. Behold, there came fire down from heaven, and burnt up the two captains of the former fifties with their fifties: therefore let my life now be precious in thy sight. And the angel of the Lord said unto Elijah, 'Go down with him: be not afraid of him. And he arose, and went down with him unto the king.

And he said unto him, 'Thus saith the Lord, Forasmuch as thou hast sent messengers to enquire of Beelzebub the god of Ekron, is it not because there is no God in Israel to enquire of his word? therefore thou shalt not come down off that bed on which thou art gone up, but shalt surely die. So he died according to the word of the Lord which Elijah had spoken. And Jehoram reigned in his stead in the second year of Jehoram the son of Jehoshaphat king of Judah; because he had no son. Now the rest of the acts of Ahaziah which he did, are they not written in the book of the Chronicles of the kings of Israel? Only an angel rescued the king's army from the fire of Elijah!

We now come to the **'Fire of Protection'** When God wants to fight for His children He sometimes uses fire. There is enough fire with God for all occasions. We see in **2 Kings 2** a chariot of fire separated the world from the spiritual: Elijah represented the heavens and Elisha the earth at that moment of separation. The two prophets stood for the two domains; heaven and earth! What a grandeur demo the Lord acted there. The chariot of fire could also have been a heavenly representative to protect Elijah on his way to the celestial city.

Powers and principalities in heavenly realms do not take lightly the events of the Kingdom. They could probably have tried their luck on his body as they did with Michael on Moses' body on the mountain. Fire comes to act as God watches over His own; may your life be surrounded with the fire of God both in this life and the one to come in Jesus' Name. It is the nature of apostolic people to be associate his fire. Oh, come fire of God! Jeremiah describes God's word as fire in his bones. David echoed the same when the word got the better of him in a spiritual experience. Almost every book there is a hint and manifestation of this fire or glory.

On another instance, the King of Babylon created a lasting legacy with their pagan famed flames and ovens of death. The story opens up like this; the pagan king was mischievously led to issue an irrevocable edict by the enemies of the Hebrews. The consequence of the edict was death by fire for the Hebrew guys who were sure to violate the edict. The king did not want to kill these men but because of pagan beliefs, oaths and edicts could not be reversed. He was tricked to it but it also suited his ego. The edict was issued that the king would set up an image in his own honor and everyone in the Republic would pay homage, (worship) to the same. Jews are commanded not to worship idols (images) of any sort so it sure was going to be a serious confrontation the wise men knew what they were doing. We see in Daniel chapter 3 the full account of this episode.

We also note on verse thirteen that the king inquired in full wrath if indeed the three Hebrew guys had disobeyed his edict. A shocking response came from the people of His fire: actual **verse 16**, the men answered the king that it was true they were not going to worship his image. It bruised the king's ego further and in a huff, he asked his hangmen to heat the furnace seven times more than usual.

When the fire was ready the king asked the army to bind the three Hebrews and throw them into the fire. They bound them as instructed and with the king furious the soldiers hurriedly did their job, but unfortunately, the heat was too much than usual for non fire people that it consumed the soldiers. It was unusual and unexpected for such to happen to trained and seasoned military personnel. Now, as the people rejoiced at the execution of disloyal foreigners while others mourned the military causalities; the king was observant as expected. The man of Judah had told him that their God would deliver them from his fire. He knew the Hebrew God but pagan systems were supposed to be fulfilled. May the fire that destroys others be for your preservation in the name of Jesus!

He leapt and went closer to the furnace to see the end of the rebels only to be met by a supernatural view; inside the fire were people walking about like they were praising and worshipping. He had tried to act a god, now God allows him to be the first to see the power of the real God. He saw what no one else was seeing, four men walking unbound inside the blazing furnace. He was shattered, confused and shaken. The fire had consumed more than twelve of his fighting men just at the mouth of the furnace, but inside the extreme heat he sees four men freely walking about unbound, unhurt yet the furnace is still red hot!

What happened? He asked his advisors an obvious question, "Did we not throw three men bound into the furnace? It was a wrong question: he was supposed to confess first that my fire has failed me today. The advisors confirmed, "Yes O King, we threw in three rebels" The king's heart tumbled. But I see four men walking freely inside the fire, only then did the rest of the people see the miracle. The king went further and preached a revelation, "I see a fourth man and he looks like the Son of Man" By the way pagans know the Son of Man but deny him. **Psalms Chapter 2 says**, ''they rage against the anointed one''. He approached the furnace entrance and with a loud voice shouted, "Shadrack, Mishack and Abednego, servants of the Most high God, Come forth, Come out here''.

Only three men came out and the fourth one we are not told by scripture wither he went. It is by correct deduction that we assume Jesus stayed in the fire or just left the pagan furnace after completing His act of deliverance to the people of the fire. All the satraps, prefects, governors, and royal advisors crowded around the three heroes of faith. They saw that the fire had not touched them, it had not hurt their bodies, nor was a hair of their head signed; their robes were not burnt nor scorched, and there was no smell of fire on them, **Dan 3:22.**

Immediately Nebuchadnezzar, learnt to praise the God of the Hebrews and against his pagan roots He made another hasty decree. From edict to decree; the anthem of pagan rulers! ''Everyone is to worship the God of the Hebrews, any failure to do so would attract death and destruction''. An edict off road with the character of our God, he was hasty and unrepentant. However the narrative clearly pits the fire of the pagans versus the people of the fire: the true God is involved and victory is for the apostolic people certain. We learn here not to trifle with the divine lest his fire breaks upon us like the soldiers of Nebuchadnezzar on that day.

Let us play close to His fire only in union, not against the God of this people, fire will consume you. Let it be known in the highways, in the spiritual territories and in the heavenly places that the God of fire and His people are untouchable. Many other fires in the Bible came as visitations, a breaking forth, a destruction, and pointer and a glorious manifestation of the heavenly domain on earth. He is a God who answers by fire; whatever the circumstances, there is fire available in commensurate measure for every occasion, a fire for every occasion;

- To my enemies – catch fire;
- To my soul – get ablaze for God;
- My gifts – burn for glory;
- To my spirit – fire of praise!
- To my friends – let the fire of God's love abound;
- To the devil and his host – fire consume you.

Jehovah is a consuming fire indeed, let us walk circumspectly, discerning His every move so that we will never be on the wrong side of His fire. He has given us everything we need for life and godliness; we cannot make excuses for want of anything. His divine power has granted unto us everything we need pertaining to the spiritual and the material. Fire becomes one of the elements provided to us of the divine to use in spiritual and physical areas. Let us connect with the fires in the right context for our benefit. When he says 'Be holy' we response in righteousness, we can do no other, after all we need him and His friendship more than He needs us. Glory.

CHAPTER 14
THE GOD OF THE APOSTOLIC PEOPLE 3
'His Fires'

All of biblical reference to fire is not without purpose. God has always had something in mind. In the Old Testament, God operated in His domain in signs, wonders and miracles. In the New Testament, he fashioned a body for himself and he operated through the agency of sinless flesh. Now, his plan is to build a church and inhabit his people with his presence and power. He has demonstrated throughout the ages that he is so interested in exhibiting his glory and power through fire more than anything else. It has always been a fire at revivals, a fire at gatherings, and glory whenever he comes to visit his church.

Let us begin these fires with **Ezekiel 36:24-27** says, "For I will take you from among the heathen, and gather you out of all countries, and will bring you into your own land. This is an agenda of election and separation of His chosen ones. **25**, 'then will I sprinkle clean water upon you, and ye shall be clean: from all your filthiness, and from all your idols, will I cleanse you. **26**, 'A new heart also will I give you, and a new spirit will I put within you: and I will take away the stony heart out of your flesh, and I will give you an heart of flesh. **27**, 'And I will put my spirit within you, and cause you to walk in my statutes, and ye shall keep my judgments, and do them" The only way this could happen is for God—who is a consuming fire - to robe himself in his church. The fire on the outside had to become the fire on the inside. No more dry walls and dry souls, we have for too long walked in the flesh, now is the time to embrace the apostolic doctrine and allow the fire of God to burn within and without.

The Psalmist said in **Psalm 104:4** *"Who maketh his angels spirits; his ministers a flaming fire."* I believe this was a veiled reference to us as his messenger ministers in the church. It's all fire, fire with God: first to flight are the angels whom we know have errands to run as ministers unto the elect and of God. But we also carry the fire within us enabling us to exhibit the plans and purposes of the divine.

Now, let's go past the major and minor prophets. Let's go past the four hundred years of silence between the Testaments. A strange figure comes out of the wilderness. His name was John. The Pharisees called him John the Baptist because he baptized his converts unto repentance. He had a new message. In **Matthew 3:11** we read,
"I indeed baptize you with water unto repentance: but he that cometh after me is mightier than I, whose shoes I am not worthy to bear: he shall baptize you with the Holy Ghost, and with fire."

Apostle John introduces the New Testament to the fire of holiness, the fire of God, the Spirit of burning and the same fire of old. He challenges his hearers to get ready for a new baptism, a baptism of fire and an infilling of the Holy Ghost. It was a baptism that only Jesus, the one who had come from the God of the fire could administer, and none other. John humbled himself and confessed that he was not even fit to untie the lace of his sandals, the one in whom dwelt the fire of baptism. Consider how great Jesus was, that this Elijah type could lower himself thus. Let us embrace and receive the fire of baptism.

We have known the Holy Ghost as living waters; but we also need to know him as the fire of God. Fire and water - water and fire, both in the same experience is a mystery of the Kingdom. Don't let this confuse you. God operates in ways we humans find contradictory. Scripture talks of the visible and invisible, of heaven and earth; of time and eternity then of flesh and Spirit. It doesn't stop there: the weak strong; the poor rich, the blind seeing etc have been viewed by some as seemingly un-flowing statements in the Holy book. Not at all, he is a God of mysteries, only the spiritually tuned can comprehend His ways the carnal mind cannot contain this. Get ready for fire baptism if you are not yet filled with Holy Spirit; open your heart and yield your all to Him, He will nourish you with the living waters which at the same time are the fire of baptism and they indwelling power that follows.

Let us scan through His fires once again: His Fire;
- The Fire of burning
- The fire of purification
- The fire of baptism
- It is the fire of judgment on sin.
- It is the fire of sacrifice.
- The fire of blessedness;
- It is the fire of the call;
- It is the fire of service.
- It is the fire of revelation.
- It is the fire of demonstration.

There is no way God can operate in you without manifesting himself as a fire. A life-changing, power-giving, miracle-working fire is necessary for a Pentecostal experience! One of the things about the holy altar fires in the Old Testament temple is that it was never allowed to go out. The tabernacle had fire burning in it continually. Even today, God has never allowed the fire go out of his tabernacle, the church. The fire in our hearts must stay aglow and that is what we mean by being led by the Spirit.

And only through prayer and praise, worship and adoration is this fire inside us kept alight.

In the book of Revelations, Apostle John describes Jesus as a fire. He tells us of Christ's whereabouts and what he looks like.

Revelation 1:12-13. "And I turned to see the voice that spake with me. And being turned, I saw seven golden candlesticks; 13; And in the midst of the seven candlesticks one like unto the Son of man, clothed with a garment down to the foot, and girt about the paps with a golden girdle." 14; His head and his hairs were white like wool, as white as snow; and his eyes were as a flame of fire'. This is why the Pentecostal church gives such emphasis to the infilling of the Holy Ghost. This need for Holy Ghost power is greater in the churches today than ever before. We face an unprecedented period of heresy, apostasy and spiritual dryness. Revival is overdue on our backslidden nation.

- Do you have the fire?
- Do you have the power?
- Do you have the baptism?
- Light the candles through prayer and never let the fire go out!

The church must have something supernatural to compensate for the flesh. It is only when Holy Spirit comes and is acknowledged that the church can claim to bear witness of the cross. Apostolic people will not settle for the average; the zeal must ignite holy fires all over. I remember this date so vividly: 7 September 1994, time 7pm at a certain primary school in a township in Zimbabwe called St Mary's in Chitungwiza. We had gathered at a partner church evening service whereby the leader was teaching a series on Holy Spirit baptism and that particular day was my day to receive the baptism of the Spirit. Surely His entrance is grand, I can reflect on my spiritual walk that the very same night was the turning point once I embraced the fire, I have never looked back nor been the same person ever again.

*Acts 1:6-8, "When they therefore were come together, they
asked of him, saying, Lord, wilt thou at this time restore again the kingdom to Israel?
7; And he said unto them, It is not for you to know the times or the seasons, which the
Father hath put in his own power.
8; But ye shall receive power, after that the Holy Ghost is come upon you: and ye shall
be witnesses unto me both in Jerusalem, and in all Judaea, and in Samaria, and
unto the uttermost part of the earth"*

Now, the challenge was to put this fire in that early church without which every aspect of New Testament worship could have no model nor inspiration. The Old had its well laid out Tabernacle and the Ark of the Covenant; the new needed Holy Spirit in order to maximize her worship experience. No child of God must move around without this in-filling of the Spirit. We are orphans without Holy Spirit baptism and His fire-some presence. Ask of Him today and right now, He comes as God's gift to His chosen, you need not work for this baptism it is a free gift of God.

Acts 2:1-4. *"And when the day of Pentecost was fully come, they were all with one accord in one place. 2; And suddenly there came a sound from heaven as of a rushing mighty wind, and it filled all the house where they were sitting. 3; And there appeared unto them cloven tongues like as of fire, and it sat upon each of them. 4; And they were all filled with the Holy Ghost, and began to speak with other tongues, as the Spirit gave them utterance."*

There is the fire! It sat upon each of them like tongues of fire, a grand entrance of the new dispensation. I don't care you believe in tongues or not, you have to because if you don't believe in one element of the Bible you are missing the mark. Anyway, whatever your approach – Receive Ye the Holy Ghost and experience, what power, what joy, what manner of life is in Him! You need Him. When the Holy Ghost makes his entrance, there is not only a rush of wind, there is also a rush of power! It's the fire that didn't consume the bush: it's the fire inside the cloud: it's the fire that shut out the fire of Nebuchadnezzar in the furnace and it's the fire of glory.

You and I need this fire. We live in a dark and cold world, the only way to avoid freezing is to fire of Holy Spirit and allow God to set our hearts ablaze. There is no way God can operate in you without manifesting Himself as a fire: a life-changing, power-giving, miracle-working fire! God has never let the fire go out of his tabernacle, even the church of which you are. Holy Spirit makes the weak strong and variant; He comes for the worthless and qualifies them for higher offices; He likes the fleeing Gideons, the disqualified Jephtas and stammering Moses'. He fills all who will open their hearts to him – everyone in the Upper Room (120) received the gift of Holy Spirit.

Accept the reality, you are a fire on the inside and that must show on the outside as you live out your in-living anointing. There is a burning bush waiting to explode inside each saved soul. I am inspired to recollect the early charismatic chorus which can inspire all of us to embrace the fire of infilling:

Fire Fire, Fire Follow Me,
Fire Fire, Fire Follow Me
On The Day Of Pentecost, Fire Follow Me.

'FIRE IN MY BONES' Jeremiah 1:1-10

Jeremiah remembers what God said to him as a boy. He shares with us a teenage memory: "Before you were born, I selected you," the Lord said to Jeremiah early in his life. "I anointed you a preacher to the nations." Not just to your congregation, not just to your denomination, not just to the Christian community, but to the world at large, to the nations, to the human community. The message you have of justice and judgment, of salvation and redemption, and of the anointing is something needed by the whole world. The message you have of truth, of peace, of beauty, of hope is a word the whole world needs to hear. Light up your fire and live out the in-living fire for the world to see God through you. You are a Jeremiah in your generation.

In these matters Jeremiah is just like Jesus. Not just that Jesus also received his call early in life. Not just that Jesus also suffered misunderstanding, torture, and rejection. For both Jesus and Jeremiah, the call was not confined to the synagogue or the temple, to the first century or the Syrian coast. Jesus and Jeremiah had a word for the world, his world and our world, my world and your world. They become our model under the anointing; we got to follow in their footsteps. 'O how God anointed Jesus of Nazareth with the Holy Ghost and with power, how He went about doing good wherever He went, delivering all who were oppressed by the devil, for God was with Him' **Acts 10:38.**

But when this word of anointing, of vocation, of calling came to Jeremiah, he resisted. He pushed it back. Jeremiah protested, "I am too young." Yet from the onset Jesus obeyed and learned from what he suffered; He even put his life at risk by telling the Jews, ''this word is fulfilled in your hearing'' after reading **Isaiah 61** in the temple. When the fire is alight you can do nothing but share, lest it burns your bones. Some of you are nervous about our age. And some of your elders want to keep you in your place. "These young people must wait their turn," one older preacher said to me in 1994, it was like an insult with what I felt then. You must honor your elders, finish your degree, receive their approval, focus on the youths, accept their time table etc. Right? In my youthful age I violated all this and who I am today is a result of obeying the fire than man's program.

Joshua 6:24; ''And they burnt the city with fire, and all that was therein: only the silver, and the gold, and the vessels of brass and of iron, they put into the treasury of the house of the Lord.
Josh 7:15, And it shall be, that he that is taken with the accursed thing shall be burnt with fire, he and all that he hath: because he hath transgressed the covenant of the Lord, and because he hath wrought folly in Israel''

Josh 8:7-8: Then ye shall rise up from the ambush, and seize upon the city: for the Lord
your God will deliver it into your hand. And it shall be, when ye have taken the city;
that ye shall set the city on fire: according to the commandment of the Lord shall ye
do. See, I have commanded you''

Joshua had the fire available to him for the occasion. There is a time to everything: the
time to set fire upon our enemies is the right time for that. *What are you going to do
with your enemies?* Set fire, like Joshua. What are you waiting for on those demonic
forces and influences that are holding you back? Set fire upon that cancer, set fire upon
that seizure abusing your child, upon that demon Loki always delaying your adventures
and ventures. Yes set fire, may my God enable you to speak forth and command the
fire of destruction, the fire of consuming and the fire of the battle.

Release blazing infernos upon that spirit of death taking young people from your
family, set fire upon the demon of addiction on the youths of your city in the name of
Jesus. Set fire. You are a people of His fire, he is a God of Fire. What a match!
It is wholly biblical to set fire upon your enemies: the Elijah deed was not a story told
by the ancients, but where God had to be called in as fire and show His hand, Elijah
did not hesitate, neither should we doubt the essence of God's fire in our generation;
either for destroying demonic forces or for preserving the covenant. And worship.

Suffer not a witch to leave, set fire upon their horses and hyenas. Set fire upon their
shrines and destroy every trace of power they may have. Set fire upon the pretensions,
the arguments and disobedience that may try to resist your progress in life. Inflict
judgment upon the devil's kingdom, yes; release judgment on every demonic spirit at
work. You have nothing to fear for no weapon that is formed against you shall
prevail, destroy, build, uproot and plant at will . You are an apostolic child – a person
of God's fire. I feel like preaching here, Glory Huh!

My Apostolic Fire Decree:
a. My God is a consuming Fire and I am also a fire.
b. Like fire Angels fly around and run my supernatural errands.
c. I am powerful, I walk in the power and fire of my God.
d. I burn all my enemies and to every demon and evil pestering my life I set fire on
    you in the name of Jesus.
e. May fire consume my enemies, not only them but their offspring and networks,
    may fire divine burn you in Jesus' name.
f. I set fire upon every weapon that has been or is being fashioned against me by the
    enemy: catch fire in the name of Jesus!

CHAPTER 15
MANIFESTATION OF THE SONS OF GOD
'Apostolic and Prophetic Realities'
19: ''For The Earnest Expectation Of The Creature Waiteth For The Manifestation Of The Sons Of God'' KJV[34]

Having explored the God of the apostolic people in the previous sections, allow us to now bring to you the manifestation of the apostolic and prophetic people. The words manifestation, exhibition, demonstration etc are the background to this whole book: how do we know the apostolic and prophetic people? How do we identify them?! The verse in **Romans 8:19** is a clear testament that we have a role to play in God's Kingdom advancement: we hold it back or move it forward. The whole of creation will only know God through us; like God were pleading with us that we shine forth on His behalf.

Once we start to manifest, we are in obedience to the command of God and meeting the expectation of all creation. This is how we reveal who we are in God. We have to be active participants of the Kingdom, as well as we reign, we serve creation and manage the earth on God's behalf. God anointed Jesus with power for ministry; the same Has He granted unto us for an exhibition of the God at work in us. We are His workmanship created in Him to do good works, so that all creation may benefit. The same way Jesus went about doing good with power is the same barometer we must use upon the apostolic people. The agenda is to deal with the devil's madness and schemes. We have the same Christ in us to go out there and deliver all who are oppressed by the devil, for God is with us. This is dominion. Demons, darkness, disease, death, dirty, and all evil will submit under an apostolic seed, let's do it!

A teacher's commentary will help us break down the lesson of **Romans 8:19**, whereby all creatures are waiting for the manifestation of the sons of God.
''All Creation Awaits'', what makes up all creation: <u>VERSE 19</u>:

    (i)   All Creation
    (ii)   Creatures
    (iii) Animate
    (iv) Inanimate
    (v)   Persons
    (vi) Angels
    (vii) Demons
    (viii) Friends

---

[34] The KJV is in Public domain

(ix)   Enemies all these make up the creation that awaits the manifestation of the sons of God. We have a demo to attend to and a show to participate in.

And what about **Eager Anticipation'**; what does the words entail – ''*Eager Anticipation*''
1. A high expectancy of a true promise, assured in essence.
2. Restless watch and wait with groaning on the inside,
3. Emotions run high as when a woman is about to give birth,(John 16:21)
4. Hope quest is visible on the faces;
5. Assurance of the promise leaves no room for any doubt;
6. Eager anticipation: even a defending undisputed champion's
blood runs high and faster before the match begins.

And lastly we look at the word **"Manifestation** in context;

- An appearing or, fulfillment;

- A breaking forth, like a shoot from dry ground;

- An imminent arrival;

- An advent, eagerly looked up to for longer time,

- To Show up, as expected;

- To demonstrate, or to prove.

- More like, a Taking over.
This is a manifestation of the sons of God for which all creation awaits with eager anticipation. We are the sons of God according to **John 1:12**. The term children of God was used in a different sense in the Old Testament as a reference to the Hebrew nation, but in the New Testament; all who accepted Jesus Christ as their personal Savior have been granted the right to become children of God. And indeed there is no other name under heaven by which we may be saved except the name Jesus – salvation is found in no other.

We are literally brothers to Jesus. We have the grace upon us to appear and takeover the running of the universe. We have to put the elephants, the lions, crocodiles and hyenas in cages; we have to travel the skies and the seas, we have no choice but to see where the sea sitteth; to travel the space and back; to burn those demons and evil spirits with the fire of God. This is they manifestation of the sons of God. We have to subdue all and conquer, we have to go to the deep and unearth the gold and the diamonds, they are all ours. It is God's glory to conceal a matter and ours is to reveal. We have to pray, praise and shake the havens and hell, and take our stand as God's offspring, all creation is calling and cheering at us so that we may come forth and appear. There is no more time to waste:

- All creation is crying: ''Rule over us''
- Even your enemies shall be your footstool.
- Shine forth sons of the Kingdom;
- Creation is waiting to see who you really are as the sons of God.
- Are you ready to rule and reign?
- Make every thought captive.
- Every demon submissive: punish them;
- Even your enemies let them hear the roar of your prayers.
- Let your presence evoke God's presence wherever you go
- Even in spiritual arenas, become part of the heavenly legislators, the council of the spiritual governors as you participate in that power wherein God has favored you with.
- Ride under the wave and anointing of Holy Spirit.

Rom 8:14:''For as many as are led by the Spirit of God, they are the sons of God'. You are now children of God through His indwelling Spirit. The same will lead you in triumph over all. **vs15**: 'For ye have not received the spirit of bondage again to fear; but ye have received the Spirit of adoption, whereby we cry, Abba, Father. **16**: The Spirit itself beareth witness with our spirit, that we are the children of God: **17:** And if children, then heirs; heirs of God, and joint-heirs with Christ; if so be that we suffer with him, that we may be also glorified together''

18: For I reckon that the sufferings of this present time are not worthy to be compared with the glory which shall be revealed in us.
19: 'For the earnest expectation of the creature waiteth for the manifestation of the sons of God''
Let the apostolic seed be not afraid of crossing boundaries, of living on the edge of faith, daring the impossible, trending the sacred, venturing into the unknown, encountering the voids, and being the change that the world want to see!
Manifest, Oh ye! sons of God; Take your stand in the Kingdom of your Father. Arise and rule, deal with resistances to your reign thoroughly. You are ordained to rule over the earth, only our dominion shall please our God. Love the Lord, love the Glory- have the glory - have the power. Let every thought be made subject to your authority in the Name of Jesus. **2 Cor 10:3-6** and like starts shall you shine and your Father will take delight in thee.

My PERSONAL APOSTOLIC & PROPHETIC DECREES

1.   I will rule and reign in the earth;

2.   I will be the head and not the tail;

3.   I will win all my battles by my God;

4.   I am a winner and not a quitter;

5.   Righteousness will go ahead of me;

6.   The Glory shall be my rearguard;

7.   All creation shall rejoice at my appearing;
8.   My prayers are being answered in the name of Jesus!
9.   My life belongs to God and not to demons.
10.   God will never leave, nor forsake me, I am dear in His sight.
11.   I shall walk in plenty and abundance.
12.   In the den of lions I shall be safe in God.
13.   Facing Jezebel may the Jehu anointing come upon me.
14.   Having sinned, may I be pardoned, and restored, may a new heart be granted to me.
15.   In lack: I shall say, ''I will see the goodness of the Lord in the land of the living''
16.   In sickness: I declare I am healed because of what the Lord has done for me on the cross.
17.   In joy: I will sing Hymns and spiritual songs.
18.   Where there is no way, I will sing, ''God will make a way; where there seems to be no way. He will make a way for me. He will be my guide, hold me closely to his side. With love and strength for each new day; He will make a way for me- He will make a way. What a song by those 90s worship singers at Integrity Music[35]
19.   When enemies mount; I will declare I fear no thing: for I have not been given a spirit of fear, I manifest great faith, great courage and great confidence because of He who is inside me.

MY APOSTOLIC& PROPHETIC PLEDGE

I …………………………...…of ……………………………… fellowshipping at ……………………………… under my spiritual father……………………………
from today.
I Commit to manifest myself in the earth as a powerful child of God,
operating and functioning in the apostolic realm for the glory of the Lord
and for my victorious living. All creation shall wait no more, Here I am! Amen.

---

[35] Integrity Music is a Music Recording and Publishing House, song God will make a way by Don Moen..

CHAPTER 16
MINDSET OF AN APOSTOLIC PEOPLE

Proverbs 23:7 is a common scripture that helps us understand that God has a keen interest in our mind and mindset in as much as everything else spiritual. As a man thinks, so is he is the Proverb. That is why He doesn't remove the brains when we get born again. But He make sure it's our responsibility to get renewed and get into conformity with the divine framework of thinking. Paul in the book of Romans brings a very interesting thought regarding mindsets;

'' I beseech you therefore, brethren, by the mercies of God, that ye present your bodies a living sacrifice, holy, acceptable unto God, which is your reasonable service. And be not conformed to this world: but be ye transformed by the renewing of your mind, that ye may prove what is that good, and acceptable, and perfect, will of God''
Romans 12:1-2

At salvation God does not take away anyone's brains, but He expects each saved soul to work towards a mind renewal. Without Christ we were going that direction, now in Christ there has to be a total reformation and transformation of the way we think. By thinking, we imply the way we use our brains, emotions, feelings, and the attitude of our hearts. It has nothing much to do with calculating algebra, or the scope to run away when a snake comes charging towards you or recognizing change shortage at a supermarket till-point. These won't change but the moral and spiritual condition alters towards godliness.

The word instructs us to be transformed, by the renewing of our minds; we have had a hard time with beliefs but now in Christ we must surrender all to Him. We have had unfaithful spirits mislead us, but now we have to transform all that to trust in the guidance of Holy Spirit, trusting as we go. This is where faith comes into effect; we enter the void by faith and navigate uncharted territories trusting Him who called us to see us through.

Even in seemingly hopeless situations, we have to trust God, not our brains; even when there seems to be no way, we have to trust God, not our common senses. We can move mountains if we dare the impossible! For with God there is no impossibility. He is too vast for our temporal struggles to limit His creative force, and it is upon us to dig deep into God so that our limitations maybe be overridden by the hand of He who has none.

Once our minds are renewed, Paul implies that it is then when we will be able to prove and know what the perfect will of God is. The carnal mind is hostile to God, neither can it accept Him. That is a key factor why we can't serve God in the flesh, it's a mockery to the whole redemption process. The flesh stands for Adam, and the Spirit for Christ, we can transit from our old self once we allow Holy Spirit to soothen our hard heartedness with the love and beauty of God.

It is true that when a man is in Christ, he is a new creature, but the new creature has some adjustments to make, some reformation to undertake, and some transition to accept. This is the work of discipleship, part of which this book was born from as I taught at COAN Gilead the Topic: Building an Apostolic and Prophetic People. The whole story of sanctification is the renewal of the mind; God through the word, the Spirit, the Christian environments chipping away at the old self so that a whole new man is complete.

Goodness comes naturally to the born again and the sanctified, but I must warn it is not automatic. I remember when I was born again, the following evening I was sitting back in my old beer drinking spot. It took strange grace that I left that beer hall without a sip, as the voice of God came to me directly warning me about the indulgencies of life. Since then I have not been perfect at all but it has been some hammering and sawing on the inside, with various recurrences of the old self, receiving warning signs from Holy Spirit and making the decisions. It is no easy a task but worth it as I can confirm that now I am living a victorious Christian life no matter all my weaknesses and the resistance of the old man (self). The decision is upon us to make: heaven and hell present choices; it's a battle for our souls and we got to take it on with a combat mindset.

"Therefore to him that knoweth to do good, and doeth it not, to him it is sin." **-James 4 vs. 17.** Here is a challenge on our part; a joy on God's part. He trusts us with our decisions and will never force anything upon us. As disciples of the cross, the elect, and the apostolic people – we have a duty to obey the scriptures, to accept the inward witness (Holy Spirit's voice on the inside) and to relate in an appropriate manner with the divine. As we renew our thinking we lean more towards obedience than rebellion, we become part of the movement of faith. We align ourselves with God's word and walk as He wills.

Our upbringing has taught us many things especially those unfortunate to have been raised in non Christian families. Doing good is not a virtue to the atheist neither is it part of the DNA of heretic religions. Repaying evil for evil is an anthem for the Hindu. Murder, killings and revenge are the hallmarks of Islam. It is not so with us; we are born of a God whose heart is slow to anger, and abounding in mercies. We serve a God who prides Himself in the art of forgiving, without his forgiveness we could still be locked up in those fiery demonic realms wherein we have been delivered.

I stumbled across some inspiring thought provoking statements that would shape us if we accept the challenge. We sit on our minds and find something or someone else to blame for lack of movement in or lives and everything. However it is upon us (as a man thinks, so is he) to work out our salvation with fear and trembling and stand the challenges of life. One teacher shared this quote while talking about the mindset: "It is better to light one candle than curse the darkness." – *Chinese Proverb.*

After complaining and blaming others for our circumstances; we must face the reality that neither height nor depth, nor things in heaven or in the earth, our age nor our color of skin; place of birth or nature of parents have any hold on our destiny. It is within our hands; in God all things have become new, the old is passed away, we have become a new creation as if we are being born for a second time with a new beginning of God's grace on our side. We love to complain that we are young like Jeremiah, but God knows us better than we know ourselves. I am too young, okay;

- Except that Jesus confounded the Pharisees and Saducees at twelve years;
- Josiah became King at eight years;
- Except[36] that Mother Teresa began her mission in India at age eighteen;
- Except that Andrew Gillum was elected a city commissioner in Tallahassee at age twenty three;
- Except that David went to war and conquered Goliath as a teenager,
- Except that Lebron James signed an NBA contract at age nineteen;
- Except that Mark Zuckerberg launched Facebook at age twenty[37];
- And that Jackie Evancho is singing like an opera star a

age ten, and worse evils are being done by little children while the righteous procrastinate doing exploits.

These kids can help us unleash the giant on the inside at any level. I heard of an eighty four year old lady who graduated with a Bachelor of Theology Degree in 2005, that's a mindset committed to a cause. We need to challenge our thinking, stretch our sets so that we will not give in nor tolerate limiting thought patterns, our destinies are to vast for small thinking. People of faith operate on realms beyond the mind, but the mind

---

[36] SWN Salem Web Network, a blogging site for various teachers of the word.
[37] SWN

must be in tune to the levels of faith desired, let we famish for want of more all the while decrying non-existent problems.

The love of comfort is what kills most of us. I call this mediocrity, loving junk. Godliness with contentment is no call to such; godliness is virtuous not average. Many of us would rather have old familiar problems than take action and face the prospect of new solutions. I have heard many say it is better to face and live with the devil you know. We have probably heard that one: that better is the devil you know, or the lesser one. May I warn you; a devil is always a devil and it is better to deal with him than to accept him. In life, we only progress when we choose to stick our necks out and dare the impossible. Go for the gold. Compromise is an art of fools when it comes to spiritual matters, there is no room for negotiation. Our souls are at stake, and eternal is the consequence to any decision taken.

The greatest pleasure we can have is to do what people say cannot be done. My learned friend Dr Fred Nana Biney[38] says, even in the hopeless situation, something can be done to succeed in his book, "How to Succeed in a Hopeless Situation" We cannot simply live in the shadows of other people. Life is real and so applies to its challenges. When we attempt the impossible, we often get the best possible result. Any person who approaches life with this attitude can be delayed by adversity but he or she cannot be denied; failure is not an option.

God knows we are extraordinary, we must agree with him within our minds. It is as he thinks, that man becomes. The extra ordinary is always risky, faith is risky, living is risky, therefore *chew the gum* or die. There are risks to any program of action but these are far insignificant when compared to the long-range risks of comfortable inaction. My good friend Onias[39] always teach pastors, "Unless we try something beyond what we have mastered we will never grow. Unless we try something that looks bigger than us, we will never experience miracles" Unless we try something extra we will never experience the extra-ordinary.

A conquered mind is operating in fear, but scripture tells us that God has not given us the spirit of fear, but of power, of a sound mind and sober judgment. [40]Most people are robbed of greatness by fear. They fear other people and their opinions. Others fear death or presumed hunger. Others just fear the feeling of fear. Fear is only real in our

---

[38] How To Succeed in a Hopeless Situation, Dr Fred Nana Biney, Rocky Hills Foundation for Human Research and Development, 1999.
[39] Onias Steve Tapera, The Lead Institute, formerly Project Leadership Africa, an NPO working with grassroots leadership development in Third World Countries
[40] KJV is in public domain, 2 Tim 1:7

minds. The only way to unmask fear is to do that which we fear and see if we are alive afterwards. Truly, ninety nine percent of our fears do not happen. Most of these fears are ridiculous when we look at them in retrospect. Greatness is not for the timid souls that prefer to interfere with no one, attempt nothing and do nothing.

To caress one's fears is to caress mediocrity. The mind requires a stretch to scrap the stench of idleness. Most people do not die because of attempting big goals; they simply expire from life with unexploited potential. The biggest form of abuse for which most of us should stand trial is "mental abuse". We use our minds for so little and just do the basic things that maintain our metabolic functions. Our minds are yearning for creative deployment not idle preservation. And they say most people at death will have just used five percent of their brain power, yes five percent at eighty years of age. We quote the great Zimbabwean teacher of Motivationals, Milton Kamwendo[41] to aid our challenge to the mindset.

Living by fear develops in man some psycho block that hinders growth and progress. Fear of anything will ultimately make reality of the negative we fear. Even motivational speakers warn against living on negativity and fear. If your faith is negative – meaning you expect negatives to happen to you, you are sinning against God, you need to repent for the perfect love of God cast away fear. And He has not given a spirit of fear or timidity, but a spirit of sound mind, sober judgment that we may live our lives as He wills.

The mind is therefore a critical component of our new life in God. The mind must be set aright to appreciate such things as are acceptable to God. Both the rich and the poor can all be successful; **Proverbs 22:2**; it goes down to the mindset. The rich who oppresses the poor is poor himself, and the poor who complains about the rich is poor indeed[42]. Employers who do not pay the right price; the rich who overeat, the powerful who oppress the weak are themselves in oppression; suffering the vice of poor mentalities and insecurity. The poor who is lazy, always complaining, and ungrateful for the little sunshine that heaven shines upon them will die in misery, never able to rise above the limitations of self indulgence.

Learn to be grateful for nature, be grateful for life, be grateful for the breath of life and you are on your way UP! Good thoughts and actions never produce bad results – try it

---

[41] Milton Kwamwendo , Zimbabwean Author of Motivational Books, owner of Innov8 A Motivational Ministry
[42] Joe Allen, as He Thinks, 1900s

over your life. **Mathew 7:18-20**, "A good tree cannot bring forth evil fruit, neither can a corrupt tree bring forth good fruit. Every tree that bringeth not forth good fruit is hewn down, and cast into the fire. Wherefore by their fruits ye shall know them' KJV.

Poverty and over indulgence are two extremes of misery both equally unnatural and both results of mental disorder. We are not rightly conditioned until we are happy.[43] Program your mindset to be happy, no-matter the circumstances it's a mental choice to be happy. Phil 4:4 seem to imply this statement, ''Be happy, don't you worry' **Phil 4:6-7**: peace is the reward of faith and trust in the creator. God wants us to be peaceful, to possess our souls by humility, peacefulness and patience **Luke 21:19**. This verse has sustained me in many battles and I rest my mind in God knowing the battle belongs to Him, and not to me. The mind works better at peace than in a huff.

We can only rise and conquer after we raise our way of thinking. And before we achieve anything spiritual or worldly, we must lift our thoughts to a certain level – Allen[44]. Any achievement is a result of effort; any effort is a result of thought in any direction – so align your thought patterns today to begin the journey to successful living. It doesn't depend on what you have or have not; who you are or are not; what happened before or what didn't happen – it all begins with a thought – as a man thinks so he becomes, **Proverbs 23:7.**

Spiritual achievements are results of holy aspirations; business achievements are results of entrepreneurial commitments; family achievements are results of social aspirations; educational achievements are results of intellectual aspirations and professional achievements are results of excellent personal approaches to work, business, recreation etc. Are you challenged; the one more word to this – ACT!

Talk your mind into submission, bring your thoughts to order: talk your fears away, talk your fears up, talk your worries away, talk your mountains faith, talk your valleys faith, as you think in your head, so shall it be. You are who you say you are: death and life are in the power of the tongue - **Proverbs 18:21**, and they that love it (*Life from tongue)*, will eat it's fruit, my emphasis. You must learn to align your thoughts and words in such a way that it will formulate whom you become. Do not be a product of hereditary or deterministic tendencies; words of the street, curses of other people's

---

[43] Allen, in As He Thinks
[44] Allen, in As He Thinks

tongues or whatever is contrary to whom you know God has made you to be. Apostolic people think like God.

The mind has potential for greatness, each mind is created great. It is upon each individual to work out how far they want to go in life. Shakespeare[45] said, "Some are born great, others greatness is thrust upon them by man, yet others make themselves great" What conclusion would you arrive at as a child of God? Are you ready for greatness? Are you ready to stretch your mind to achieve your goals? To think as Christ would like you to, so that you can form an indestructible partnership for Kingdom exploits. As a man thinks, so is he, it is from within that primary greatness shall be attained leading to all greatness.

As long as God is the centre of your life, you cannot be stopped. Evil will be far from you. You carry an original anointing that enables you to go beyond the limits. What the mind cannot do, the anointing takes over, what the mind is limited to, the grace exceeds. Remember our God; He is able to do exceedingly, abundantly, above all that we can think or imagine according to His power that is at work in us. Let this enlighten us as apostolic and prophetic people so that we make the most of our earthly lives, to the glory of the Lord.

---

[45] Othello, William Shakespeare

CHAPTER 17
MONEY AND THE APOSTOLIC PEOPLE

Ecclessiates 10:19

This message was shared at the *SUPERNATURAL SHIFT 4 EXPLOITS CONFERENCE* Hosted by COAN Gilead International Ministries in Johannesburg at the Royal Faith Tarbenacle, in September 2017. This section will address the contentious issue of money and the apostolic people. Many would like us to believe that money is the root of all evil, but we are wiser enough to know what the Bible says. An ancient said, 'the rich think that the greatest need in the world is love, but the poor know its money'.

"For the love of money is the root of all evil: which while some coveted after, they have erred from the faith, and pierced themselves through with many sorrows.'' 1 Tim 6:10. It says, "the love of money'' not necessarily money in itself. So we can conclude that attitude towards a thing, not the thing in itself creates the spiritual problem. Our theology, then, requires reconfiguration to teach exactly what the Bible is saying about money. And after all, it is wrong to build a doctrine on one scripture or try to attach a meaning to a text whereas it has its meaning already.

Our approach to money has serious implications on both our spirituality and material lives. There is no separation that should be put between the two aspects of our lives; those who compartmentalize their lives into the material, spiritual, social etc would soon realize it's a waste of time. Life is a one indivisible whole. God should always be at the center of our lives whether be it in business, ministry, and family: everywhere the key to success and victory is to have God at the centre of everything.

I shared in the previous chapter about the challenge for greatness; our conditions we find ourselves in are a result of past actions. We may be victims of other people's failure to plan or we are our own product. Deterministic tendencies are the reason for fools; great people override their histories with a new framework of thinking and a shift in paradigm. If you want something to change, change it and if you want your world to change, you change it. Money can play a significant role in your endeavors to better your world, it answers a lot of questions.

We can refer you to Shakespeare again regarding greatness: born great, made great by other man, or made self great. These are the only three parameters of greatness. But primary greatness is self made; it comes from intrinsic value, and inherent aspirations.

Good intentions accompanied by good actions produce good results. There is no variation. Here are the greatness parameters:

♦ Born with It- Inheritance, default status;
♦ Made so By Man - Corporate Grace, or
♦ Self Made – Reformed thought patterns or shift in perspective on life.

I am convinced I belong to the last parameter; I have labored my whole life to be who I am today. I do not minimize the efforts of my parents, teachers and lecturers during my formative years but how rough life has been, how hard I have tried, and how wide I have conquered: I want to say I have made myself great and no one in this world can claim they have made me who I am. In all this, God is the centre. How I conduct myself in the grace has produced the author of this book, and lets all say, 'to God be the Glory'

A look at our **1 Chronicles 12:14**- The Gaddittes, a generation with exquisite talent and with a spiritual heritage, expanded by skill and discipline. These people have now been famed for their artistic competencies, and the Bible has indicated that they are heroes in the Kingdom of God. It is from generation to generation that important articles of life differ. In our time we need money. The secret about money is the key to success. **Eccl 10:19** says, ''Money answers all things''. You will agree with me that Scripture is not saying wisdom, prayer, anointing, spirituality, hard-work etc on this text: it says, Money.

And what is money? Money is an undisputable medium of exchange. Measured by how much you attract - ideas, what you do when you have it - investment, your attitude towards it - the entrepreneurial spirit, and your philanthropic appreciation. Currency speaks of flowing; when you become the destination of money you are finished in growth terms. As a man thinks, so is he, *even around money, emphasis mine,* **Proverbs 23**:7 - biblical thinking refers also to the business of the head, heart and soul not brain works only.

Back to money: having or not having is not the subject; our behavior around it matters. Money is a resource that everyone is after, but the secret which everyone isn't aware of is that money don't just come to everyone. No-matter how hard you work, or how much you stress or how thrifty you are in pursuing it. It is attracted by the environment one would have created. Instead of pursuing money, pursue an idea. Why, because money follows ideas. This means money should be looking for you, not vice versa.

Take a deep look at how money circulates from one person to the other. If you do not have an idea it will not come your way. Money doesn't stay in one pocket, or on one person. Why? Because no one owns money, no one has power over money, even the billionaires know this. The only thing that has power over money is an idea. *An idea is the power of humanity over money*. Hear this apostolic people; when you have an idea you attract money, but it does not mean to say you are going to have it forever. Keep improving; keep upgrading your idea because money is attracted to the best idea.

The Bible says, "Whatever your hand finds to do (idea) do it with all your might'' (focus) therein money comes running. Do it. Do it. Just do it with all your might, *emphasis is mine*. We have been schooled to pray, to fast and to do other religious practices, but when it comes to money all those practices become no different to wishes, this I have learnt by experience and the hard way.

We can safely say, an **IDEA + ENTREPRENEURIAL ACTION x WISDOM = SUCCESS.** This formula works in any environment. Even conmen sell ideas, and then money flows in! Hahaha! Careful: reality has taught us. That is why people believe that money comes and goes.

To the elect it must always be money cometh; I have learnt this secret to my confession from Gloria Copeland. Her teachings about attitude towards money really helped me revisit my approach to success and prosperity. If you want to have money and success in life be a problem solver. Look for problems and turn them into opportunities. There are a lot of successful businesses that fell because of lack of new ideas on how to upgrade and improve their departments. Every rich and successful person started with an idea that was then worked on **Proverbs 10:4** says, "lazy hands maketh poor''

The clothes we wear started as an idea in someone's head, these chairs we sit on started as an idea, the light bulb started as an idea, everything else started as an idea, so there is a need to come up with an idea before money. Money is the last thing to consider because it follows our thoughts. The most critical thing needed in life to be successful is not money or anything material but just an idea. The power of meta-physical planning cannot be underestimated. And ideas are very rare; our worldview of life is littered with complains and laziness.

Laziness defined: Laziness is resting or wanting to rest before doing anything; eating without working, expecting harvest where no seed was sown, looking out for miracle money while living a holy-less life, and unscriptural convictions like; God helps those who help themselves, if I miss God's tithe He will understand, I am poor God knows that the rich are the ones supposed to give, the earth is an unfair territory. All this is spiritual garbage.

No-matter what lenses we use, God will not give in and make some humanly nice convictions to be part of His holy writ. *Nada! Bodo!*[46] The entire SHIFT must happen on our side. Take a deep look into your life and be true to yourself: How many ideas did you come up with and how many have you pursued? Don't blame the economy or anyone; blame yourself and your thinking. Your thoughts have made you! Change the way you think and start thinking positively about your life and make progress.

Any significant breakthrough in history has been a result of a daring break with traditional ways of thinking. The tendency to blame others is very easy, but that of doing better is challenging. Walk your Talk and thoughts to the bank and stop blaming God for what He didn't do; even Satan has not done all that you blame him for around the issue of money.

Apostolic people, is there an idea we can bless and anoint? My name is

_____ and I have a great idea to

....

....

.........., that I desire God to bless and anoint my mind for execution in Jesus name. I am going to be fruitful, prosperous and successful in it to the glory of my God.

God blesses the works of your hands, a result of the thoughts of your mind (ideas) and focus - an ingredient to achievers' cycle. Stop working for nothing. Stop prioritizing Pharaoh's ideas and have your own. Greatness is possible if we can Shift from traditional ways of thinking. *Anoda kunyengererwa, Anoda kukumbirwa kuti azvishandire;* Whoever is lazy; whoever has no idea, *Popanda Nzeru*[47] ...... you become your own worst enemy. Your Idea is your Future! SHIFT your perspective. Money is always hidden behind an idea! SHIFT your focus and realign your priorities. We all need money, others want it more, even those who do not preach about it they

---

[46] Nada – Portuguese, Bodo – Shona fro NO
[47] Chichewa – where the brains are not working

are busy scheming behind the schemes to live or simply make ends meet. Let's be honest with each other; mother is a requisite for life as the Bible mentions it.

MY APOSTOLIC & PROPHETIC MONEY DECREES

- I am Shifting, I am changing my pattern and ways.
- I confess today that money shall follow me.
- I am abounding in ideas and the grace to execute.
- I am due for seed of the sower from above.
- I will work my bread without toiling.
- I will have the right perspective with money.
- I am the seed of the righteous; whatever I touch shall prosper in Jesus' name.
- No-more to mediocrity;
- No-more to laziness;
- No-more to complaining about my circumstances.
- No-more junk upon my life, money cometh!

CHAPTER 18
THE COVENANT AND APOSTOLIC PEOPLE
'The Tithe Debate'

It would be injustice to this project to conclude without attending the issue of apostolic giving. We have a call to give to God in many ways as instructed by scripture. Let us explore the subject as we close. There is no subject to attend than the Tithe Debate' as we play our part in training the masses in the ways of Jehovah. We will dwell on scriptural references that can help the apostolic and prophetic people understand the doctrine of the tithe.

2 Tim 3:16; ''All Scripture is inspired by God and is profitable for teaching, for rebuking, for correcting, for training in righteousness, so that the man of God may be complete, equipped for every good work''. If it says all scripture, then we have no choice but to take heed and obey giving instructions in as much as we obey all the other scriptures. Some biblical giving is even a command as we shall see in the exploration ahead.

Romans 15:4, 'For whatever was written in the past was written for our instruction, so that we may have hope through endurance and through the encouragement from the Scriptures' We can do no other, we are bound by the word of God as apostolic people, we are people of the word. Let us now turn to the tithe debate and offer our contribution from a yes to the tithe perspective. I have heard about one pastor in South Africa who 'does not believe' in the tithe. Convictions differ, but scripture should not be steer-wrestled to mean what we feel or prefer. I hundred percent don't agree with him and I feel sorry for that pastor and his church as they are missing out on a very enriching spiritual practice. Tithing is a test of trust and obedience.

Deut 8:10-18, ''When you eat and are full, you will praise the Lord your God for the good land He has given you. "Be careful that you don't forget the Lord your God by failing to keep His command — the ordinances and statutes — I am giving you today. When you eat and are full, and build beautiful houses to live in, and your herds and flocks grow large, and your silver and gold multiply, and everything else you have increases, be careful that your heart doesn't become proud and you forget the Lord your God who brought you out of the land of Egypt, out of the place of slavery. He led you through the great and terrible wilderness with its poisonous snakes and scorpions, a thirsty land where there was no water. He brought water out of the flint-like rock for you. He fed you in the wilderness with manna that your fathers had not known, in order to humble and test you, so that in the end He might cause you to prosper. You may say to yourself, 'My power and my own ability have gained this wealth for me,' but remember that the Lord your God gives you the power to gain wealth, in order to confirm His covenant He swore to your fathers, as it is today''

Here is a call to remember the Lord. It looks like the Law of Moses here was persuasive; unusual with the Mosaic law, it usually was command after command. God offers a persuasive plea to the chosen nation to remember the tithe as a covenant keeping practice. The implication of these verses above is that one who does not tithe is saying, ''all I have I gained by my own strength'. God has no place in the heart of the man who does not remember him through the tithe. Malachi brings the command and demand aspect and we will do well take heed lest we live our lives exposed to the locust and the pestilence.

Gen 1:28-30, 'God blessed them, and God said to them, "Be fruitful, multiply, fill the earth, and subdue it. Rule the fish of the sea, the birds of the sky, and every creature that crawls on the earth." God also said, "Look, I have given you every seed-bearing plant on the surface of the entire earth and every tree whose fruit contains seed. This food will be for you, for all the wildlife of the earth, for every bird of the sky, and for every creature that crawls on the earth — everything having the breath of life in it.

I have given every green plant for food" And it was so, God blessed them, and God said to them, "Be fruitful, multiply, fill the earth, and subdue it. Rule the fish of the sea, the birds of the sky, and every creature that crawls on the earth." God also said, "Look, I have given you every seed-bearing plant on the surface of the entire earth and every tree whose fruit contains seed. This food will be for you, for all the wildlife of the earth, for every bird of the sky, and for every creature that crawls on the earth — everything having the breath of life in it. I have given every green plant for food." And it was so. We can see that all that we have is from God, the power, the wisdom, the ability even to create wealth is God given. Who are we then to refuse to give him the ten percent he demands of us.

The primary call of man is to be a blessing, just as God is a blessing through and through. Our introduction to all creation is the endowment of blessedness. Before any other instruction we were given the garden to manage and enjoy the blessing of peace and sufficient providence. So, the doctrine of blessings is scriptural, real and original.

Gen 12:1-4a, ''The Lord said to Abram: 'Go out from your land, your relatives, and your father's house to the land that I will show you. I will make you into a great nation, I will bless you, I will make your name great, and you will be a blessing. I will bless those who bless you, I will curse those who treat you with contempt, and all the peoples on earth will be blessed through you. So Abram went, as the Lord had told him, and Lot went with him. Abram was seventy five years old when he left Haran'' The narrative:

- Leave your family, your land, your people – the blessing is in obedience;
- I will bless thee – a vow by God, an unalterable decree;
- I will make your name great – there will be visible manifestation of your blessedness;
- You will be a blessing – you don't seek blessings, you become the blessing;
- Whoever blesses you I will bless – God in oath, ties Himself in covenant.
- Whoever curses you I will curse – His covenantal protection.

Let's develop further: **Genesis 14:1-20**, ' '*In those days Amraphel king of Shinar, Arioch king of Ellasar, Chedorlaomer king of Elam, and Tidal king of Goiim waged war against Bera king of Sodom, Birsha king of Gomorrah, Shinab king of Admah, and Shemeber king of Zeboiim, as well as the king of Bela (that is, Zoar). All of these came as allies to the Valley of Siddim (that is, the Dead Sea). They were subject to Chedorlaomer for 12 years, but in the thirteenth year they rebelled. In the fourteenth year Chedorlaomer and the kings who were with him came and defeated the Rephaim in Ashteroth-karnaim, the Zuzim in Ham, the Emim in Shaveh-kiriathaim, and the Horites in the mountains of Seir, as far as El-paran by the wilderness. Then they came back to invade En-mishpat (that is, Kadesh), and they defeated all the territory of the Amalekites, as well as the Amorites who lived in Hazazon-tamar''*

- ♦ The Kings represent domains to be conquered and dominions to be captured as outstanding heritage.
- ♦ Battles of life are won with God on our side- not aligning with the Princes of this world.

♦ Do not stay in Sodom, it's a land of laziness, faithlessness and strange happenings.
♦ If you stay in Sodom you will lose everything you have worked for.
♦ The blessed are sustained and preserved, they can also save the Lots.
♦ Abram was Blessed and powerful, look at **verse 14** after the survivor reported Lot's capture;
♦ Do not be a Sodomite or you will be captured as Lot was, be an active believer.

Now verse **17-18** takes us to the subject of the Tithe, indeed it is a mystery. Mysteries are very powerful spiritual components of the faith. Abraham worked, fought, captured and won a resounding victory. He never forgot the power that helped him win his victories: nay, he gave a tithe. So all who claim to be descendants or children of Abraham by faith must show in their attitude towards the tithe; your father was a tither.

Gen 14:17-18, ''After Abram returned from defeating Chedorlaomer and the kings who were with him, the king of Sodom went out to meet him in the Valley of Shaveh (that is, the King's Valley). Then Melchizedek, king of Salem, brought out bread and wine; he was a priest to God Most High. He blessed him and said: Abram is blessed by God Most High, Creator of heaven and earth, and I give praise to God Most High who has handed over your enemies to you. **20**. 'And I give praise to God Most High who has handed over your enemies to you. And Abram gave him *A Tenth Of Everything*'' setting an example for all who would be his descendants as sand on the shores and the innumerable stars seen that night of visitation.

A Tenth of Everything

Luke 11:42, ''You give a tenth of mint, rue, and every kind of herb, and you bypass justice and love for God. These things you should have done without neglecting the others. You give a tenth of mint, rue, and every kind of herb, and you bypass justice and love for God. These things you should have done without neglecting the others'' So Jesus is here confirming the tithe must be given without ignoring other spiritual duties.

How our generation loves to do all other spiritual duties, but the tithe is a sign and a potent. The tithe is a serious test; it requires surrender, consistency and transparency that is why many avoid the subject at many turns. Here is a true test of obedience and

129

trust, God promises to kick out the devourer on what is left on our side, that ninety percent: do we believe He will do it? We can do no other – a tenth of everything!

Mathew 5:20, ''And I tell you, unless your righteousness surpasses that of the scribes and Pharisees, you will never enter the kingdom of heaven''. These are the guys who tithed even their garden produce, the herd and grain, everything they accumulated was due a tithe, and Jesus says, our righteousness (our power to do right and obey God) must exceed them and this is a New Testament doctrine.

Hebrews 7:1-10, ''For this Melchizedek - King of Salem, priest of the Most High God, who met Abraham and blessed him as he returned from defeating the kings, and Abraham gave him a tenth of everything; first, his name means king of righteousness, then also, king of Salem, meaning king of peace; without father, mother, or genealogy, having neither beginning of days nor end of life, but resembling the Son of God — remains a priest forever. Now consider how great this man was that even Abraham the patriarch gave a tenth of the plunder to him! The sons of Levi who receive the priestly office have a command according to the law to collect a tenth from the people — that is, from their brothers — though they have also descended from Abraham. But one without this lineage collected tenths from Abraham and blessed the one who had the promises''

''Without a doubt, the inferior is blessed by the superior. In the one case, men who will die receive tenths, but in the other case, Scripture testifies that he lives. And in a sense Levi himself, who receives tenths, has paid tenths through Abraham, for he was still within his ancestor when Melchizedek met him''

These are Kingdom secrets that require understanding; no-one will understand unless there is a teacher of the word. The greater blesses the lesser when tithes are being surrendered to the Lord. The apostolic people understand this that the tithe is received by their spiritual leaders, who in turn invoke the Abrahamic blessing that always accompanies the giving of the tithe. Each believer must have a family to where they belong, in order to be consistent in the giving of this tithe and be asked questions in the absence of faithfulness. There has to be accountability so belong to a church!

This Mezchezdek we see meeting Abraham was Jesus Christ pre-incarnate. Jesus was a Levite, who by then was still in Abraham's bosom when the tithe was given. Abraham gave Melchezdek the Tithe in honor of Jesus who would later appear to him at Mt

Moriah at the sacrifice of Isaac. There is need for a blessing to be invoked at the giving of the Tithe that is why the tithe goes upwards.

Abraham blessed God after giving the Tithe: you also must bless God whenever you give your tithe. The mystery of the tithe is the Covenant, The Oath to Bless, the protection in redemption, the Blessing of the Greater: who is the greater we represent! What is your response to all this: The Tithe is paramount in sustaining the Covenant, and a bargain with God. **Malachi 3:10**.

Malachi 3:6-12: 'For I am the Lord, I change not; therefore ye sons of Jacob are not consumed. Even from the days of your fathers ye are gone away from mine ordinances, and have not kept them. Return unto me, and I will return unto you, saith the Lord of hosts.   But ye said, 'Wherein shall we return?
Will a man rob God? Yet ye have robbed me. But ye say, 'Wherein have we robbed thee? 'in tithes and offerings. Ye are cursed with a curse: for ye have robbed me, even this whole nation''

''Bring ye all the tithes into the storehouse, that there may be meat in mine house, and prove me now herewith, saith the Lord of hosts, if I will not open you the windows of heaven,
and pour you out a blessing, that there shall not be room enough to receive it. And I will rebuke the devourer for your sakes, and he shall not destroy the fruits of your ground; neither shall your vine cast her fruit before the time in the field, saith the Lord of hosts. And all nations shall call you blessed: for ye shall be a delightsome land, saith the Lord of hosts''

The Hebrews had a model response to God's call for their gifts and sacrifices. We will conclude with an inspiring shout from the Hebrews in the book of Nehemiah: **Neh 10:35**, 'We will bring the first-fruits of our land and of every fruit tree to the Lord's house year by year. We will also bring the firstborn of our sons and our livestock, as prescribed by the law, and will bring the firstborn of our herds and flocks to the house of our God, to the priests who serve in our God's house. We will bring a loaf from our first batch of dough to the priests at the storerooms of the house of our God. We will also bring the first fruits of our grain offerings, of every fruit tree, and of the new wine and oil. A tenth of our land's produce belongs to the Levites, for the Levites are to collect the one-tenth offering in all our agricultural towns'.

A priest of Aaronic descent must accompany the Levites when they collect the tenth, and the Levites must take a tenth of this offering to the storerooms of the treasury in the house of our God. For the Israelites and the Levites are to bring the contributions of grain, new wine, and oil to the storerooms where the articles of the sanctuary are kept and where the priests who minister are, along with the gatekeepers and singers. We will not neglect the house of our God' God be with you all as you begin to tithe, your choice, your voice, your obedience to the scriptures. Apostolic people do tithe – do you?

Here is a model response for the apostolic people; what a joy to hear the chants of the Hebrews confirming that they will do what the Lord asks regarding their first-fruits, their sacrifices and offerings. Another version says, "Far be it from us to neglect the house of our God' When the house in neglected, we have poor pastors who are not a model for unbelievers to wish to join the church. When tithes are neglected, ministers create unorthodox means of raising funds for ministry and for their welfare. When the House of God is neglected, even the expansion of the Kingdom of God suffers. The resources required for ministry must come from within and from without the church.

Even governments should consider the Western system whereby grants are made available to true churches so that the salt and the light of the world will not be hampered by resources. Governments cannot change the hearts of the people; they have no power to make good people no-matter how good they govern. It is the duty of true churches to touch hearts and moderate the moral condition of the society; that calls for every government to support the churches. If civic society and non-governmental organizations get grants, there has to be a stipulated percentage for the true church, because we go to the heart of man and provide a different but crucial need for humanity: God, good, and goodness.

On top of the tithes and offerings, we need God fearing governments to take note and act. This will unleash a blessing upon the government itself and the nation at large. Social ills are limited when people understand the will of God for man, not when NGOs are multiplied. Crime is an issue of both the economic environment and the heart, but primary to it is the condition of people's heart. The church has been placed by God to reach out, to teach, to touch and heal those very hearths. So, rise up apostolic people and do great exploits for your Father's Kingdom. A Tenth of Everything!

CHAPTER 19
DOCTRINE AND THE APOSTOLIC PEOPLE
'The Convictions'

"As I urged you when I was going to Macedonia, remain at Ephesus so that you may charge certain persons not to teach any different doctrine, nor to devote themselves to myths and endless genealogies, which promote speculations rather than the stewardship from God that is by faith. The aim of our charge is love that issues from a pure heart and a good conscience and a sincere faith. Certain persons, by swerving from these, have wandered away into vain discussion, desiring to be teachers of the law, without understanding either what they are saying or the things about which they make confident assertions"
1 Tim 3:1-7 ESV

The Apostolic Creed is a sure starting point to define and explain the doctrinal convictions of the apostolic people's convictions. Many would argue about the Roman influence on this creed but it sure stands the test of time in providing a basic foundation to apostolic convictions. Forget about the Roman Church, focus on the doctrines, you will agree with us that it will lead us to Him. We will however open up with the New Testament teachings that support and clarify these convictions.

The foundation for our faith is the advent of Christ, His manifest in the flesh (incarnation). We accept His persecutions, His trial and judgment and His death on the cross for our guilt. Then comes His burial, His resurrection and His final appearance to the disciples become the divine acts for our salvation and deliverance. These form the background to any true Christological doctrine. Without that death and resurrection, the Christian faith is doomed.

"For all have sinned, and come short of the glory of God; Being justified freely by his grace through the redemption that is in Christ Jesus: Whom God hath set forth to be a propitiation through faith in his blood, to declare his righteousness for the remission of sins that are past, through the forbearance of God; To declare, I say, at this time his righteousness: that he might be just, and the justifier of him which believeth in Jesus"
Romans 3:23.
It is true all have sinned, as in the sin of Adam (rebellion against God). And the wages of sin is death: the second death which experienced only by those who have not believed in God's only way of salvation. And this salvation is found in no other: 'Neither is there salvation in any other: for there is none other name under heaven given among men, whereby we must be saved' **Acts 4:12**. Apostolic people are convinced that it is only through Jesus that we can know and come to God.

He said it Himself during His days on earth: *"Jesus saith unto him, I am the way, the truth, and the life: no man cometh unto the Father, but by me. If ye had known me, ye should have known my Father also: and from henceforth ye know him, and have seen him. Philip saith unto him, Lord, shew us the Father, and it sufficeth us. Jesus saith unto him, Have I been so long time with you, and yet hast thou not known me, Philip? he that hath seen me hath seen the Father; and how sayest thou then, shew us the Father?"* **John 14:6-9** KJV[48]

We have become children of God by believing on the One He sent; we are adopted through the New Birth and He gives us His Spirit by whom we cry Abba Father. We are unstoppable because we belong to God. Our adoption is cause for celebration because without Christ we are all dead to God. We are not a religion as Christians; we are the truth: all other religions have no sure confession regarding God, they have a thin connection to their gods who be not gods at all, others still even mock the substitutionary death, taking Christ's death for granted. As apostolic people we are not ashamed to be called God's children according to the Bible from which ninety percent of the world's religions copy uncharacteristically.

Acts 2:41, 42:
'Then they that gladly received his word were baptized: and the same day there were added unto them about three thousand souls. And they continued steadfastly in the apostles' doctrine and fellowship, and in breaking of bread, and in prayers'

This text sums up the doctrinal behavior of an apostolic people. After salvation we are baptized into the commonwealth of God's people. Then we undergo discipleship at the feet of our leaders. Steadfastly brings a picture of serious dedication and commitment to the same. True believers share everything in common and have the passion to partake of the sacraments of Christological doctrine.

Ephesians 4:14, 15:
That we henceforth be no more children, tossed to and fro, and carried about with every wind of doctrine, by the sleight of men, and cunning craftiness, whereby they lie in wait to deceive; But speaking the truth in love, may grow up into him in all things, which is the head, even Christ,

Discipleship and training in righteousness is the only antidote for doctrinal error. It is imperative that the spiritual fathers in any generation take time to teach, to write books

---

[48] The KJV is in public domain

and literature to preserve the doctrine. There is a trick the enemy uses to deflect the truth over the years, like cancer he slowly neutralizes the truths of the word and each generation has a challenge to resist and defend the faith. Even our much acclaimed modern Biblical versions are taking the hearts away from the truth little by little in contemporization. Each believer must learn to study the Bible and to stand for what it teaches in any circumstance. We must be Bible taught and Spirit taught as A.W Tozer puts it in his Gems from Tozer[49].

The word of the early prophets carry weight in our doctrinal interpretation; the prophet Isaiah and the other prophets foretold the coming of Christ ages before it came to pass. The fulfillment is sufficient evidence of the veracity of the Bible prophecies and the Book itself. It is no secret that we are a prophetic kingdom, a God generation, a God people, and a people whose faith is set in eternal domains. How to explain the accuracy of the Messianic prophecies is a no-brainer because everything happened as the prophets foretold; thus as God planned it out.

We can touch on redemption and deliverance; much is at stake in the pages of each biblical book. Our healing is from the wounds inflicted upon Jesus during the torture and shameful abuse by the Jews; and our deliverance was wrought in hell; where Christ spent three nights after death disempowering the powers of darkness right in their own backyard. I like it as put forth by preachers that Christ tormented Satan in hell immediately after death; He went in there and even preached the good news of salvation, such that some long dead souls heard him and were resurrected and were seen walking in the streets of Jerusalem. **Mathew 27:51.**

There was so much power that Satan gave up all he had stolen after the garden episode. He had to give up the keys: the keys of life and death; the keys of hell and the keys of life on earth our Champion Jesus recovered in those days he was in the heart of the earth. Not only had prophets foretold; Jesus Himself had told His followers that as Jonah was three days in the heart of the earth so shall the Son of Man be.

What a type with Jonah: Jonah was an evangelist in the same way Jesus evangelized beyond Hell. What could have been Jesus' mission in the grave for three nights apart from dealing with Satan! He claimed in **Luke 10:19**, ''I saw Satan falling down like lightning. Behold I have given you authority, to trample down snakes and scorpions (devils) and to overcome all the power of the enemy and nothing will harm you" This was also another victory prophecy of Christ regarding the victorious Christian life designed for every born again child of God.

---

[49] Bible Taught and Spirit Taught, Gems from Tozer. Paternoster Press 1999

We can do nothing but marvel at the unfolding of events around His crucifixion and death; Jesus indeed was killed, and he was buried and He rose again. Without rising from the dead we could be another one of the world's religions. But, watch it, He rose and the killers confirmed it, the saints confirmed it, the angels confirmed, and to deal away with any doubt He appeared, first on the road to Emmaus and then to His disciples and then to about five hundred chosen ones. This is the root of our confession. Glorious Christ!

We declare and decree that Jesus came for us:
- He lived to establish my way to follow – doctrine;
- He was wounded for my transgression; substitution.
- He died for my salvation, so that I do not have to die twice; mercy.
- He rose for my victory and vindication; deliverance.
- He went to heaven as an eternal testimony; divine.
- I am powerful, He has given me authority, and I am a threat to the devil; anointing.
- Not only a threat but my life is gonna be a scourge to the enemy's kingdom;
- I will plunder hell and populate heaven;
- I will live for the Kingdom and;
- All creation shall see my manifestation as an apostolic and prophetic child of the Most High God.

"And from us at Sunday Moring Literature and GileadVEST Corporation we say, "Reading through this Book is a sign that you are a seeker of the Kingdom; seekers find. May the Kingdom and its righteousness be your portion beginning now and forever. May you walk always in plenty, always in victory, with apostolic and prophetic graces surrounding you. May you always in power and always with God walk in multiple miracles. Rise up apostolic people, let not the cult and crass enjoy the goodies of your father while you wallow and winnow in oblivion. Align your convictions to these truths and reap the rewards of victory.

Creation is waiting with eager anticipation for your manifestation as sons of God. Arise and make the difference the world yearns to see. We are of God; we are divine offspring and nothing shall separate us from the love of God. This is our conviction, this is our victory, this is our confession, these are our convictions.
To God be the Glory, and honor and the power, forever and ever. Amen.

CONCLUSION
''For all creation awaits with eager anticipation for the manifestation of the sons of God''
'Romans 8:19'

'Here We Are' we have responded!

Let us do these things as we exhibit the love, the beauty, the glory and the power of our God. There is joy in pleasing God. Creation shall see and wonder; the earth shall behold and open up its voices to honor the King because of us. Let us send the praise, the worship, the hymns and spiritual songs in their billions and this world shall know, that there is only one true God and that He has a people on earth; an apostolic and prophetic specie: a people of His fire, a people of manifestation and demonstration of His might. We are rulers; we reign in the earth as Kings and Priests unto our God.

We are a people He calls His own; therefore we declare:
- Christ died and rose for us, we are His ambassadors.
- We will manifest ourselves as sons of the living God.
- We operate and function without fear in the Kingdom for we have not been given the spirit of fear.
- We are a people of His fire: let the fire of God burn on the inside and outside.
- I will do with fire what I see my father do!
- I am royalty; my dominion extends beyond the eye.
- No eye have seen, nor ear heard what the Lord has planned for me. I operate the prophetic because of the one who is inside me.
- My God is a consuming fire: he consumes my enemies.
- Like a lion strong, so am I, Oh' like a lion.
- I decree victory and success, I cannot fail.
- My tithe will preserve my covenant and to me I prophesy- money cometh.
- I am a willing participant to sacrificial living in the Kingdom of God.
- I am supernatural; natures bows. There is no sorcery or divination that works against me.
- Never again shall I be the devil's victim.
- Never again shall I be the devil's pillow.
- Never again shall I be the devil's puppet! Never again!
- I confess and agree: I am Powerful, Classy and Supernatural because of Christ.

BIBLIOGRAPHY

King James Version of the Bible; Olive Tree Online Edition.

Holman Edition of the Bible. Olive Tree, Online Edition.

English Standard Version of the Bible. Olive Tree, Online Edition
NIV Study Bible, Zondervan 1995.

How to Succeed in a Hopeless Situation, Fred Nana Biney, Dr, 1999.

Success Unlimited, Cardwell Nyaungwa, Amazon Kindle 2015

Dickson Teachers' New Testament, Rodger E Dickson.

 As He Thinks, Joe Allen.

Marks of a True Church, Cardwell Nyaungwa, Amazon Kindle 2012.

Grace That Conquers, C. Nyaungwa Amazon Kindle, 2014

Sermons by Dr Cardwell Nyaungwa, E-Files.

Salem Web Network

Supernatural SHIFT for Exploits Conference, 1-3 September 2017, @ COAN Gilead's Royal Faith Tabernacle; JNB South Africa.

AW Tozer, Gems from Tozer, Paternoster Press 1999.

OTHER BOOKS BY THE AUTHOR

Dr CL Nyaungwa - Ministering

1. CONFLICT MANAGER, a Leadership Toolkit on Conflict Management
2. MARKS OF A TRUE CHURCH
3. THE MIRACLE TALK SHOW
4. SUCCESS UNLIMITED; The Ethics
5. THE ECONOMY OF THE CROSS
6. FAITH THAT CONQUERS
7. THE MYSTERY OF GRACE
8. WORTH MORE THAN A SPARROW
9. NOT A CHURCH BUT A CULT, Exposing the Largest Cult in the Universe
10. DIASPORA REALITIES, publishing yet
11. THE MAKING OF A DICATATOR, publishing yet

LET'S TALK BUSINESS AND MINISTRY

BLOG: Wordpress.com/Doccn.   Face-book: Apostle Cardwell Nyaungwa.

Instagram;   drcardwell nyaungwa

Twitter: Doccnnyaungwa.   LinkedIn: dr cardwell nyaungwa.

YouTube: Dr cardwellnyaungwa. www.nyaungwaconsultant.Business1.com.

www.ingramcontent.com/pod-product-compliance
Lightning Source LLC
Chambersburg PA
CBHW030536130626
46552CB00006B/2292